"You look like you had a close encounter with a hard object."

Against the pallor of her skin, Cindy's irises were an even more startling blue than Scott remembered. A sudden, unexpected urge to reach out and take her hand in a comforting clasp swept over him.

"I was cleaning out a clogged gutter and the ladder tilted. I fell, hit my head and blacked out. What are you doing here?"

Scott gave her a recap of Gram's situation. "She's had a rough year and a half. My grandfather died, she broke her hip and had to move into assisted living. I'm not sure how many more setbacks she can take."

Cindy's eyes softened in empathy. "That's a lot of trouble to deal with all at once."

"Yeah." He raked his fingers through his hair, considering his next move. Might as well take the plunge. "Do you need a ride home?"

Cindy blinked. "Um…thank you, but that's too much of an imposition. I can call a friend."

No mention of a husband.

Don't push, Walsh. It's none of your business.

Books by Irene Hannon

Love Inspired

IRENE HANNON

is an author of more than thirty-five novels. Her books have been honored with two coveted RITA® Awards (the Oscar of romantic fiction), a HOLT Medallion, a Daphne du Maurier Award and two Reviewers' Choice Awards from *RT Book Reviews* magazine. *Booklist* also named one of her novels a "Top 10 Inspirational Fiction" title for 2011. A former corporate communications executive with a Fortune 500 company, Irene now writes full-time from her home in Missouri. For more information, visit www.irenehannon.com.

Finding Home

Irene Hannon

Love Inspired

Recycling programs
for this product may
not exist in your area.

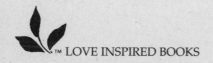 ™ LOVE INSPIRED BOOKS

ISBN-13: 978-0-373-81644-6

FINDING HOME

Copyright © 2012 by Irene Hannon

www.LoveInspiredBooks.com

Printed in U.S.A.

Those whose steps are guided by the Lord,
whose way God approves, may stumble,
but they will never fall,
for the Lord holds their hand.
—*Psalms* 37:23–24

To Tom—
As we celebrate 23 years of marriage.
May the magic continue!

Chapter One

The kid was back.

Again.

Putting himself in danger.

Again.

Bracing against the gusty March wind on The Point, Scott Walsh squinted at the blond-haired boy. He was ten, maybe eleven. The perfect age to be tempted by all the heavy equipment on the Northern California headland. Twenty-five years ago, that could have been him. He, too, would have found the allure hard to resist.

But empathy didn't equate to tolerance.

He flexed the fingers of his left hand and glanced down at the scars crisscrossing the back, the shiny white lines and limited mobility a constant reminder that when it came to safety, he couldn't afford to be Mr. Nice Guy.

Lips clamped together, he switched his focus

back to the boy. The kid had been smart, waiting until the crew called it quits for the weekend before venturing out here. He'd also managed to elude the off-hours security guard, though that wouldn't have been difficult. The long-retired Humboldt County deputy was more show than substance, his presence intended to deter rather than enforce.

The boy's back was to him as he examined the bucket on one of the giant excavators, then proceeded to check out the crawler treads that were as tall as he was. Last time he'd spotted the kid, Scott had yelled at him from across the construction site. The youngster had taken off before he got close.

He wouldn't make that mistake again.

Scott wove through the obstacle course of equipment, trenches and lumber, where all of the foundation work for the upscale inn had been completed on schedule—as promised. Meeting deadlines was a sticking point with him and a hallmark of Walsh Construction. It was also one of the reasons Mattson Properties had chosen his firm to tackle the high-profile project. Not a day passed that he didn't give thanks for this opportunity—and the much-needed income it was providing.

The wind in the needled branches of the spruce and hemlock trees, along with the muted crash of surf on the rocks below the towering headland, masked his footsteps as he approached the excavator. He'd like nothing better than to grab the boy by the scruff of his neck and haul him back to his negligent parents. But touching him wouldn't be smart. The parents could sue him for assault if they were ticked off. He'd have to settle for getting in the kid's face and putting the fear of the Almighty into him.

Not until his shadow fell over him did the boy realize he had company. By the time he spun around, Scott was only two feet away.

The youngster's panicked gaze darted left, then right. He whipped his head around to look behind him, but the excavator treads cut off that avenue of escape.

Scott invaded his space, placing his hands on the treads on either side of the boy's head to pin him in. Long enough, he hoped, to get his message across.

"I thought I told you two days ago to stay out of here."

The boy stared up at him in silence, eyes wide, face colorless.

"Construction sites are dangerous. And so is this stuff." Scott banged a hand against the metal body of the excavator above the kid's head.

The boy flinched and folded his body into a protective tuck.

Then he started to shake.

Scott frowned. He'd dealt with plenty of curious kids on job sites in Eureka, and most had been defiant. As a result, he'd ramped up his tough-guy stance over the past four years. But this wasn't a big city like Eureka, where gangs and drugs caused problems. The only gang in tiny Starfish Bay was probably the group of seniors who met every Wednesday morning at the Mercantile's coffee nook to OD on caffeine.

A twinge of remorse tugging at his conscience, he softened his tone a fraction, eased back a few inches and planted his fists on his hips. "What's your name?"

The boy might be scared, but he was thinking clearly enough to see his opening. Instead of responding, he lunged past Scott and tore off for the woods, legs pumping, dirt flying.

Scott stayed where he was as he cupped his hands around his mouth. "If I see you around here again, I'm going to call the county sheriff!"

The boy cast a terrified look over his shoulder and kept running. Thirty seconds later, he disappeared behind the sheltering branches of the coniferous trees that separated the headland from the town.

Scott waited a full minute, then pulled his keys from his pocket and set off for his SUV.

He'd flag Al down on his way out and alert the guard to be on the lookout for trespassers. But he had a feeling he'd seen the last of the blond-haired interloper.

Mission accomplished.

Still…the image of the boy's frightened face nipped at his conscience. Maybe he'd gone a little overboard with his intimidation tactics.

He stopped beside his SUV, transferred his keys to his left hand so he could open the door—and watched them slip to the ground before his fingers could close over them.

Expelling a frustrated breath, he bent to retrieve them. And as the dipping sun illuminated the shiny white spiderweb of lines on his hand, his lips settled into a resolute line.

He didn't like scaring kids—but if fear kept the boy safe, Scott could live with the guilt.

"Did something unpleasant happen at school today?"

Cindy Peterson cut a bite of the Orchid Café's famous pot roast and speared it with her fork, struggling to keep her tone conversational as she addressed her son. His reticence, his subdued manner, the way he was picking at his food—it was all a flashback to a year ago, reminding her of the weeks of grief counseling, her sleepless nights of worry, his slipping grades. But they were past that, weren't they? *Please, God, let us be past that!*

"No."

She watched Jarrod poke at the mashed potatoes he usually inhaled. "You're very quiet tonight."

He shrugged.

Okay. Time to regroup. Think this through with her head instead of her heart.

Jarrod had had two big tests this week. It was possible he was just tired. She certainly was. The Humboldt County Historical Society worked with a lean staff at the best of times; losing one person had had a ripple effect on everyone. Cindy hadn't liked staying late every night for the past three weeks or leaving Jarrod alone for an extra couple of hours after school, but what could she do? She needed this job— and right now, it needed her more than usual.

Perhaps she was overreacting. It may simply have been a long week for both of them.

"Would you like to watch a video tonight? I could make some chocolate chip cookies, too." She forced herself to lift the fork to her mouth and chew the piece of pot roast that had grown cold.

"I guess."

Bad sign. A video and cookies always elicited enthusiasm.

The wad of meat got stuck in her throat, and she reached for her glass of water to wash it down. Took a long swallow. Inhaled a calming breath.

"Jarrod." She waited until he lifted his chin. "Why don't you tell me what's going on?"

He wrinkled his brow. Indecision clouded his eyes, but he remained silent.

"Did you have another run-in with Mark?" The class bully had chosen her son as a target a few months ago, further upsetting him for weeks. The little tyrant might be on the warpath again.

"No." He gave his potatoes another listless poke. Let out a long sigh. Slanted a look at her. "It's no big deal, really. I know I promised to stay inside after school, but I got tired of being cooped up." His grip tightened on his fork, and he licked his lips. "So tonight and Wednesday I went out to…"

He stopped abruptly. Stared over her shoulder toward the café entrance. Paled.

Swiveling in her seat, Cindy checked out the small foyer. A tall man in dirt-smudged jeans and work boots stood inside the entrance, a snug T-shirt outlining his broad shoulders and impressive biceps as he surveyed the crowded café.

Behind her, a fork clattered to the floor. Her son dived for it as she turned.

When he lingered below the table, she furrowed her brow and leaned sideways to check on him. "Jarrod? What's going…"

"Excuse me."

As the male voice spoke, a pair of well-broken-in work boots appeared in her field of vision.

Cindy righted herself and found the man from the foyer standing beside their table. His glowering scowl suggested he had a temper to go with his dark auburn hair.

But why would a stranger be angry with her?

The man shot a quick look at her left hand, adorned only by a slender gold band. "I assume the boy hiding under the table is your son?"

His accusatory tone stiffened Cindy's spine, and she straightened in her seat. "He's not hiding. Jarrod, sit back in your chair. We'll get you another fork."

Her son slowly emerged from below the table, avoiding eye contact with her. That evasive maneuver, plus the telltale flush on his cheeks, set off warning bells in her head.

"What don't I know here?" She focused on Jarrod, but the stranger spoke.

"I caught him trespassing on The Point twice this week. I warned him the first time. Today, I threatened to notify the sheriff. But a mother will do for now. Keep him away from the construction site. I don't want any accidents on this job. Got it?"

Warmth crept over Cindy's cheeks as her own anger spiked. "You don't have to be rude about it."

He flicked a glance toward the bulging briefcase on the seat beside her. "I do when parents don't take responsibility for their kid's safety."

His jab at her parenting skills stung.

But it also produced a twinge of guilt. She hadn't been as diligent as usual in the past couple of weeks, thanks to her job. And she didn't want her son wandering around a dangerous construction site any more than this man did. Whoever he was.

"It won't happen again."

"Good."

"Here you go, Jarrod. I saw you drop yours from across the room." Genevieve Durham came bustling over, waving a clean fork. She set it beside Jarrod's plate and beamed at the new arrival, patting a stray wisp of white hair back into place. "Hello, Scott. Having dinner?"

"I was, but I think I'll head home instead. It's been a long week. And not all of it pleasant." He shot Cindy and Jarrod a narrow-eyed look.

"I'm sorry to hear that. I understand things are moving along on schedule at the inn, though. That's a positive."

Genevieve and her sister, Lillian, could charm a smile out of almost anyone with their perennial upbeat attitudes. Cindy wasn't surprised they'd made a rousing success of the Orchid. But the charm didn't work on this man.

"Yeah." His lips remained flat.

If Genevieve was aware of his bad temper, her sunny demeanor gave no indication of it. "Well, you drive safe and have a nice weekend."

"Thanks. I'll try."

Without even glancing again toward mother and son, the man departed.

Genevieve adjusted her glasses, propped her hands on her ample hips and inspected the plates on the table. "You two haven't made much progress on my pot roast tonight. Did I forget to put in a spice? Are the potatoes undercooked?"

"No. It's wonderful, as usual." Cindy wadded her napkin in her lap. "But we both had a busy week. I think we're just tired."

"Busy, busy, busy. The story of modern life." The older woman huffed out a breath. "That nice young man is forever on the run, too." She gestured over her shoulder, toward the door where Scott had disappeared. "Eats so fast he hardly warms a chair—but I guess overseeing a job like Inn at The Point is a big responsibility."

"Is he the foreman?" Cindy took a sip of

water, keeping one eye on Jarrod. His guilty flush told her he was dreading their upcoming one-on-one conversation.

"Among other things. He's eaten breakfast or dinner here a few times, but he doesn't talk a lot about himself. I do know he owns Walsh Construction. A few of the guys on his crew stop in for breakfast on occasion, and from what I've overheard, he almost lives on the job site. And he's very conscientious and safety-oriented." Genevieve checked out their plates again. "Would you like some take-out cartons?"

"That would be great. Thanks."

"Coming right up."

As Genevieve moved away, Cindy pushed her plate aside, rested her forearms on the table and folded her hands as she regarded her son. "You want to tell me your side of this?"

"I was starting to tell you when he showed up." He shot her a defensive look.

"Okay. Go ahead and finish."

"I got done with my homework early on Wednesday and tonight. I know you told me to stay inside, but I'm tired of being alone in the house every night. It's boring. I didn't think anyone would care if I went down to The Point to look at the trucks and stuff. Nobody's there after four, except the guard, and I didn't hurt anything. I don't know why he got so mad."

The mere thought of her son wandering around among all that huge equipment sent a shiver through her. "He got mad because you were trespassing—and because a construction site can be dangerous."

Jarrod broke off a piece of the roll and crumbled it on his plate. "It's not dangerous if you're careful. And I didn't touch anything."

"A place like that can be dangerous even if you're careful. You're lucky Mr. Walsh didn't follow through on his threat and call the sheriff."

Her son bowed his head. "Yeah. I guess. I won't go back anymore."

Cindy could tell he meant it. Now. But if he got bored again—or adventure beckoned—the temptation might be too strong to resist.

"Maybe I need to think about aftercare again until school is out."

"Aw, Mom." He shot her a stricken look. "I'm gonna be twelve in two months! I'm too old for a babysitter! I won't go back. Honest. I don't like that guy, anyway. He's mean."

Yes, he was. But Cindy kept that opinion to herself as she pinned her son with her strictest, cut-no-slack look. "Is that a promise, Jarrod?"

"Yeah."

"Okay. I trust you to keep it. But you did break our rules by going in the first place. You know there are consequences for that. What do you think would be a fair punishment?"

"No TV for three days?" His expression was hopeful.

"Nice try. Let's make it a week because you broke the rules twice."

His face fell. "I guess that means no video or cookies tonight either."

"No video, but I think the cookies would be okay."

His demeanor brightened a few watts. "Awesome!"

"Here you go." Genevieve rejoined them and set two lidded disposable containers on the table. "That pot roast will heat up real fine in the microwave tomorrow for lunch."

"We're gonna make cookies when we get home," Jarrod offered.

"Now that sounds like a fine activity for a Friday night. You two have fun." With a lift of her hand, she hurried over to seat some latecomers.

As Cindy transferred their food to the two boxes, Jarrod propped his elbow on the table and settled his chin in his palm, his face thoughtful. "I wonder if that guy has any kids."

"Why?"

With one finger, Jarrod traced a ring of water left on the table by his glass. "I kind of feel sorry for them if he does. I bet he wouldn't take them on hikes in the redwoods or help them bake cookies. He isn't anything like Dad."

Cindy swallowed past the sudden tightness in her throat as she scraped the last of the carrots into the second container and locked the lid in place. "No, honey, he isn't. Ready to go?"

"Yeah."

Her son slid out of his seat, and as they wove through the tables toward the exit, she, too, felt sorry for the man's children—if he had any.

And for his wife.

Because living with a stern, bad-tempered construction company owner who she suspected rarely laughed would be no picnic.

Scott stopped outside the assisted-living facility to take one last, deep breath of the crisp salt air. Over the past eleven months that exercise had become a ritual, an attempt to psyche himself up for the distinctive and unappealing aroma that clung to Seaside Gardens—and every facility like it. An unsettling combination of death, age, excrement, disinfectant, mass-produced food and air freshener.

He'd checked out half a dozen of the finest such facilities in Eureka, and the obnoxious smell was omnipresent. It was even here, at the best of the best. It would be one thing if there was no choice; he could cope better with that. But Gram didn't belong here.

Trouble was, she thought she did—and she was as stubborn as he was. Once she'd decided this was where she was going to die, nothing he or the doctors or the counselor she'd sent packing had tried had convinced her otherwise. Including prayer.

Nevertheless he persisted, closing his eyes to repeat the words he said before every visit.

Lord, give me strength. Show me how to reach her. To lift her spirits. To give her hope.

Straightening his shoulders, he stepped inside, nodded to the evening receptionist—and kept walking. Mandy would talk his arm off if he gave her half a chance. After almost a year of daily visits, he knew most of the employees—by design. As he'd discovered, even in an upscale facility like this, the staff was more attentive to the depressingly small number of residents who had regular visitors.

He paused at his grandmother's door, hoping he'd find her sitting in the easy chair in her private room, dressed in the capris and soft knit sweaters she used to favor, reading one of those romance novels he'd always teased her about. He'd supplied her with plenty of them over the past few months—yet all of them remained untouched in a sack in the corner of her room.

Instead, the scene was the same as it had been last night. And the night before. And the night before that.

Barbara Walsh was in bed, dressed in a cotton housecoat, the sheet pulled up to her chin. Her eyes were closed. Her hands were folded on top, at her waist.

She was still as death.

Shaking off that depressing thought, Scott scanned the room for clues about her day. Her half-eaten dinner tray rested on the beside table; she hadn't bothered to go to the dining room for her evening meal. Her walker was out of reach; she hadn't used it except to go to the bathroom—with assistance. Her Bible lay unopened on the nightstand beside her; she hadn't turned to it for comfort, as had been her practice in the old days.

Conclusion? No transformation had happened in the past twenty-four hours. Not that he'd expected one. But he hadn't given up yet, even if she had.

He moved beside the bed and touched her shoulder. "Hi, Gram."

Her eyelids fluttered open and she blinked at him, as if orienting herself. "Don't you have better things to do on a Friday night than visit an old lady in a nursing home?"

At least her mind was still sharp.

"There's nothing I'd rather be doing."

She snorted. "Then you're the one who needs a doctor, not me. You're a young, handsome man. You should be out on a date." Her words were sassy, like in the old days, but her tone was listless.

"Thirty-seven isn't that young."

"It is when you're seventy-seven, like me." She peered at him. "Why don't you patch things up with Angela? I bet she'd take you back."

Discussing his former girlfriend wasn't on his agenda for the evening. "Did you walk today?"

"You're avoiding the subject."

"That's right." He retrieved the walker and set it beside the bed. "Let's take a stroll."

"I'm too tired."

"You always say that."

"That's because I'm always tired."

"You wouldn't be if you moved around more. Exercise energizes."

"You're going to badger me until I get up, aren't you?"

"Yep." They had the same discussion every night.

"Fine. Let's not waste a lot of breath arguing. I'll need it for this marathon walk you always insist on."

She threw back the covers and with his help

swung her legs to the floor, stood and steadied herself on the walker.

"I hate this thing."

"If you'd go to physical therapy, you wouldn't need it. A broken hip doesn't have to be disabling."

"I did go to physical therapy. It hurt. And I didn't get any better."

"It's supposed to hurt—and you quit too soon. Rehab takes time."

"I don't have time." Her tone was flat. Resigned.

Scott blew out a breath and counted to five. "Gram, you're only seventy-seven. The doctors all say you could recover and go home if you put some effort into it."

"Home to what?" She gripped the handle of the walker as a spasm of grief twisted her features and her shoulders slumped. "Without Stan, it's just an empty house."

That was the crux of the problem, Scott knew, as he guided her toward the door and started down the hall beside her. Gram had never recovered from his grandfather's death a year and a half ago. After fifty-five years of marriage to her best friend, the loss had been devastating. And after falling and breaking her hip, she'd given up.

"The house isn't empty at the moment."

She shot him a distressed look. "I feel terrible about that, too. Giving up your apartment to save money just to pay for this place..." She shook her head. "I don't know why the good Lord doesn't take me. Everyone would be happier."

"I wouldn't be."

"You'd have your life back."

"Gram." He stopped and faced her. "You're a major part of my life."

"I shouldn't be. And I wouldn't be if you still had Angela. You've never told me what happened, but I bet she got tired of you always running over here to see me instead of taking her out. Not to mention spending a fortune on a lost cause when you could have used the money for a down payment on a nice house."

Shock rippled through him. "Is that what you think?"

"What else could it be? You two went out for close to three years."

He raked his fingers through his hair. "You had nothing to do with our breakup. There was just something...missing. I should have ended things a lot sooner than I did."

Skepticism narrowed her eyes. "Is that the truth?"

"I've never lied to you."

She conceded his point with a nod. "True

enough. Since the day your parents died and you and Devon came to live with us, you've never given me a lick of trouble. That overdeveloped guilt complex of yours always kept you in line, prodded you to do the right thing. Like waste a lot of time with an old lady."

"Love is why I'm here, Gram. Not guilt."

"Sometimes those two can get tangled up."

"Not in this case."

A sheen appeared in her eyes, and she patted his hand. "Nice to know. But then again, you've always been a good boy. Always had your head on straight. Which is more than I can say for your sister. She called today, by the way."

"She must need money."

"She does—but she knows better than to ask me for it these days. If I were you, though, I'd be expecting a call."

"What's her story this time?"

"She had to cut back on her waitressing to go to a bunch of auditions, so she got behind in her rent. Something about a new off-Broadway play she's being considered for that could be her big break."

"In other words, the usual." Scott had always admired Devon for chasing her dream, but after ten years the emergency pleas for cash were getting old. "I hate to say it, but if she hasn't gotten her break by now, I doubt she ever will."

"I told her the same thing this afternoon. She wasn't happy."

He chuckled. "I can imagine." His sister had the same red hair he did—and a temper to match. "What did she say?"

"Among other things, she implied I was being rude."

Rude.

The word echoed in his mind as his grand-mother launched into a blow-by-blow account of her conversation with his sister. That boy's mother had called him rude earlier, at the café, and he supposed he had been. But he'd always been a straightforward, call-'em-like-I-see-'em kind of guy. Especially when he was aggra-vated.

"Are you listening to me, Scott?"

His grandmother's question pulled him back to the present. "Sorry. My mind wandered for a minute."

"I noticed. We've gone far enough anyway. I'm getting tired."

He didn't protest as she turned back toward her room. They'd covered more ground than usual. "If you walked several times a day, you'd build up your stamina and endurance."

"So you keep telling me. However, I'm more interested in where your mind wandered. It's not like you to get distracted."

"I know. It's kind of weird." He told her about finding the boy on the construction site and his encounter with mother and son in the restaurant earlier in the evening, glossing over the in-your-face tactics he'd used.

"You've never belabored an incident like that before. Safety trumps everything—including good manners—according to you. I wonder why this little run-in bothered you."

She posed it as a rhetorical question, and he didn't bother trying to answer.

But as he got his grandmother settled for the night, kissed her forehead and walked outside, the question lingered.

And suddenly, as the image of angry sky-blue eyes flashed across his mind, he had his answer.

It wasn't the anger that had bothered him, however. It was the deep-seated hurt lurking just below the surface. The boy's mother had looked like a woman who'd endured her share of challenges and heartaches. A woman who didn't need any more stress piled on her slender shoulders.

Yet he'd dumped another load of it on her.

The overdeveloped guilt complex Gram had mentioned earlier reared its head as he walked toward his car. Yes, the kid had been out of line. Yes, his parents had been negligent. He'd had every right to confront the mother. His zero tolerance for danger on the job site was completely justified.

However...he could have been more diplomatic. Used a bit more finesse.

He opened the door, slid behind the wheel and inserted the key in the ignition. He needed food, not regrets. Why lament a situation he couldn't change? All he could do was try to be nicer and make amends should their paths cross again.

And for some reason he found himself hoping they did.

Even if it required eating a little crow.

Chapter Two

"Do you have a minute?"

At the query from her boss, Cindy took a surreptitious peek at her watch before she looked up from her piled-high desk. 4:58 p.m. So much for the resolution she'd made over the weekend to leave on time. It had lasted all of one work day.

"Sure. Have a seat. Let me move that stuff out of your way."

She started to rise to clear the chair on the other side of her desk, but Elaine waved her aside. "This baby may be slowing me down—" she patted her six-months-pregnant bump "—but my arms work fine." After depositing a box of old photos on the floor, she lowered herself into the seat. "I have good news and bad news. I'll lead off with the bad news. Sarah handed in her resignation this morning."

Cindy blinked. "Wow. Two resignations in one month?"

"It's a first—and not a happy one for us. Sarah's husband got a job offer back East. He's already gone, and she wants to follow ASAP. We've got her for two more weeks. I'm glad he finally connected somewhere after being unemployed for eighteen months, but it's a bummer for us. The hours are long enough here as it is."

"Tell me about it." Cindy surveyed the boxes and files that covered her desk and lined the walls in her small office.

"That brings me to the good news. I have candidates lined up for both empty positions. The woman I interviewed this morning will be an excellent fit for Brett's job. We're going to make an offer this week."

"What about Sarah's job?"

Elaine folded her hands over her rounded stomach and grinned. "How would you like a promotion?"

A few beats of silence passed as Cindy digested the unexpected offer. "I've only been here a year."

"But you came to us with excellent credentials from your museum work in Dallas."

"That was twelve years ago."

"You haven't lost any of your skills. I was

sorry I couldn't offer you a higher-level job to start with. Now I can."

When she named the new salary, Cindy caught her breath. She and Jarrod were doing okay, but the extra money would help. A lot.

"That sounds great, Elaine. Thank you."

"Exemplary work deserves to be rewarded. However…there is a downside. I know you've been trying to keep regular hours, and I understand that. You've had some rough months, and Jarrod needs you. But as the collections and displays manager, you'll be responsible for the Summer Sizzler exhibit. Because you're new in the job, the project will probably require extra hours. Is that a problem?"

Was it? Cindy had helped Sarah last year with the display for the annual fundraising drive. It had been complicated and time-consuming, but six years of doing it had allowed Sarah to pull it off with ease—and do a stellar job. "Barnstorming, Balloons and Blimps" had chronicled area history from a bird's-eye perspective, garnering widespread media attention and encouraging generous—and much-needed—contributions from residents.

Topping that would be tough.

But with the fundraising kickoff only five months away, a pro like Sarah would surely have things well under way. She could make this work without too many extra late hours if she skipped her lunch breaks and came in earlier.

"It's not a problem." She gave Elaine a confident smile. "And thank you for the opportunity."

"Thank *you*. I'm glad I had someone well-qualified close at hand. Because I'll be out playing new mommy—" she tapped her tummy "—I won't be much help. But I know you'll do a great job."

"I'll meet with Sarah tomorrow to go over the project."

"Perfect." Elaine hoisted herself to her feet. "Now go home. While you can."

As Elaine disappeared through the door, Cindy shut down her computer and stuffed some documents in her briefcase to review after Jarrod went to bed, still marveling over the unexpected promotion. Not a bad way to end a Monday.

Yet as she grabbed her purse, doubt began to erode her euphoria.

Had she taken on too much? With life just settling down for her and Jarrod, was it wise to throw in a new complication? Should she have turned down the offer?

She slung her purse over her shoulder and gripped her briefcase. She'd already been putting in extra hours thanks to the short-staffed situation, so that was nothing new. And she and Jarrod were coping, despite last Friday's glitch with that unpleasant Scott Walsh. Plus, it wasn't as if she'd have to start from scratch on the exhibit. She could build on whatever Sarah had already worked up. By next year, after a full twelve months in the job, she'd be ready to tackle the project on her own. She had the skills. The enthusiasm. The confidence of her boss.

There was no reason to worry.

Twenty-four hours later, Cindy pulled into the parking lot at the Orchid to pick up take-out dinners, set the brake, rested her forehead on the wheel—and fought back another wave of panic. They'd been crashing over her steadily since nine o'clock this morning, when she'd discovered Sarah hadn't even begun to work on the display proposal yet.

What had she gotten herself into?

She wanted to be angry, but how could she be after Sarah had admitted her husband had been fighting depression for months? That she'd been on edge for weeks while he advanced from one round of interviews to another for his new job? That her doctor had prescribed an antianxiety drug to help her cope? Worry could short-circuit thinking processes, derail sleep and wreak havoc in a life. Cindy suspected it was a huge challenge for Sarah just to get through each day without falling apart. She could empathize.

Been there, done that.

But the display proposal was due in three weeks, and none of the preliminary ideas in the thin folder Sarah had handed her were strong enough to pursue.

She swung open her car door and slowly filled her lungs with the spruce-scented air. Exhaled. Repeated the exercise as she stood. In. Out. In. Out. The calming technique had never failed her.

Until tonight.

Short of backing out of the job she'd accepted twenty-four hours ago, she was locked into much longer hours than she'd anticipated. There was no recourse if she wanted to come up with a blockbuster exhibit—and that meant she wouldn't be around as much for Jarrod.

Nerves frayed, she slammed the door. Why were the good things in life so often double-edged swords?

Genevieve spotted her the minute she stepped through the door beneath the gaudy purple-flowered sign, her usual sunny smile in place. "I'll have your dinners right out. That was a smart idea to call ahead." The older woman cocked her head as she scrutinized Cindy's face. "Tough day?"

"I've had better."

The older woman tut-tutted. "I'll throw in a couple of brownies on the house. They might help sweeten things up."

Cindy managed to coax her lips into the semblance of a smile. "Thanks."

"My pleasure." Genevieve waved toward the handful of chairs lined up against a wall in the foyer. "Have a seat. I'll be back in a jiffy."

A man in jeans and a cotton shirt, his hair more pepper than salt, smiled as Cindy approached, then picked up his hard hat from the one vacant chair. "Popular place."

"Always." She sat beside him.

"Worth the wait, though. The sisters sure know how to cook. I'll be sorry to see this job end, even if the commute is a bear."

She eyed the hat. "You're working on the inn, right?"

"Good guess." He grinned and held out his hand. "Win Griffith. I'm the project manager for Mattson Properties."

She returned his firm grip. "Cindy Peterson. You must work with Scott Walsh."

"Every day. Are you two acquainted?"

"We met Friday." Her blood pressure spiked

at the thought of her encounter with the rude construction company owner.

The man beside her pursed his lips. "I'm not picking up positive vibes. Was there a problem?"

"Let's just say politeness isn't his forte."

He frowned. "What happened?"

"He caught my eleven-year-old son on the construction site after hours. Twice. I'm not excusing Jarrod's behavior, and the matter has been addressed, but I didn't appreciate being accosted in a public place about the issue."

The twin furrows on the man's brow deepened. "I'm very sorry that happened. Mr. Mattson has made it clear he wants to have a positive relationship with the town and its residents. That directive has been passed on to all the contractors."

Suddenly Cindy regretted her heated words. She had a feeling Scott was going to hear about her complaint—and she hadn't intended to get him in trouble. If she hadn't been stressed by her own job situation tonight, she'd have thought before speaking.

Time to backtrack.

"He might have had a long day. That happens." She summoned up a smile. "And I'm glad he's diligent about keeping kids off the site. I'm sure the last thing Mattson Properties wants is an accident."

"True. But that doesn't excuse rudeness."

"Here you go, Win. Enjoy that meat loaf." Genevieve hustled over, handed him a take-out carton and leaned closer, dropping her voice. "I added an extra piece, too. After being out in the fresh air all day, I'm sure you've worked up a big appetite."

"You and Lillian are going to spoil me." Win rose and grinned at the white-haired woman.

She waved his comment aside. "We like to keep our friends happy."

"So do we." Win included Cindy in his response, strengthening her suspicion that Scott Walsh was in for a talking-to. "Good night, ladies." With a dip of his head, he walked toward the door.

"Such a nice man." Genevieve sighed as he exited, then smoothed out her ruffled apron. "I'll have your dinners out next, Cindy."

"No hurry." Cindy crossed her legs. Resettled her purse in her lap. Tried to focus on her challenge at work as Genevieve disappeared into the kitchen.

But thoughts of a man with red hair kept distracting her. Scott Walsh hadn't struck her as the kind of guy who put up with a lot of grief. Or who was used to getting his hand slapped.

Come tomorrow, though, she was pretty certain he was in for a healthy dose of both—thanks to her.

And given his over-the-top reaction to Jarrod's transgression, that temper of his was about to get another workout.

The muscles in Scott's shoulders tightened, and his fingers clenched around the edge of the hard hat in his hand as he stared at his boss across the desk in the cramped construction trailer. "She complained about me?"

"Not without some prompting. She made a comment that raised a red flag and I pressed her." Win leaned back in his chair, his posture relaxed, his tone conversational.

But he wasn't relaxed. Scott had been working with the man for three months. When Win had a serious matter to discuss he was calm, rational—and brutally honest. If someone messed up, he told them straight out. There was no pointing fingers, no ranting. He just laid out the facts, listened to the other side and ended the conversation with an admonition to do better.

Scott had admired his style and tried to emulate it. But he'd failed big-time on Friday night——and Jarrod's mother had made certain his boss knew all about it.

Thanks a lot, lady.

"You want to tell me your version?"

At Win's prompt, Scott counted to five, wishing he had time to get to ten. "I don't have much to add. Like she said, the kid trespassed—twice. I ran into them at the Orchid, and I told her to keep him off the site."

"She's still upset about your…conversation."

An image of weary blue eyes flashed across Scott's mind, and a twinge of guilt tugged at his conscience as he thought about the encounter that had been more confrontation than conversation. "I guess I could have been more diplomatic."

Win let a few beats of silence pass, showing Scott he concurred with that assessment.

The man leaned forward and folded his hands on his desk. "Mattson wants any problems handled with kid gloves. There was a lot of opposition from town residents to this development in the beginning, and he doesn't want to incur any more enmity."

Scott knew that. He'd met with Louis Mattson when the developer had been reviewing construction company bids for Inn at The Point, and once hired, Mattson had given him the skinny on the town's resistance and told him there was also a PR component to the job. He wanted to keep Starfish Bay residents happy, not tick them off.

"I'm sorry." He had to dredge up the words. Apologizing had never been his strength—as Gram often reminded him.

"I don't want kids on the site, either, of course. And I want this job finished with a clean safety record. But let's see if we can deal with these kinds of problems in a less in-your-face way, okay?"

"Okay." Heat rose on his neck. "It won't happen again."

"I'm sure it won't. And if you get the chance, see if you can make things right with Cindy Peterson."

Looked like he'd be eating crow after all. "I'll do my best."

"Good enough. Now let's get back to work."

As Scott rose, his cell phone began to vibrate. He waited until he was outside to check caller ID, giving his temper a few seconds to cool.

Once in the sunlight, he glanced down.

Devon.

He fisted one hand on his hip. This was her second call in the past twenty-four hours, and he'd let it roll to voice mail last night. Might as well deal with this latest appeal for emergency funds while he was still hot under the collar and less likely to cave.

Pressing the talk button, he walked toward the edge of the headland, where a fine mist rose from waves crashing against the rocks below. "Good morning."

"It's noon here." He heard her stifle a yawn. "But it feels like morning."

"Late night?"

"Some of us got free tickets to a new play and we went out for pizza afterward. I decided to sleep in for… What's that noise? Are you at Gram's?"

Scott had grown so used to the barking seals that he'd tuned them out. "No. I'm on the job site. We have a seal colony on the rocks below us." One of his excavator operators gestured him over, and he walked toward the man. "I've got to run. Did you have a specific reason for calling?" Like he didn't know.

"Uh…yeah." She gave him the same story she'd relayed to Gram about being up for a new part and having less time for her waitress job. "So I was hoping you could spare a few bucks to tide me over."

It was her usual breezy request. More assumption than appeal. He'd heard it a hundred times. In the past, he'd just forked over whatever amount she needed. Like Gram and Gramp, he'd been so grateful she'd been spared in the car accident that had taken the lives of their parents that he'd spoiled her rotten through the years. As a result, she'd come to believe cosseting was her due.

But for some reason today her attitude rankled him. Maybe he should follow Gram's example. Tell her to take some responsibility for her life. Everyone else handled their own problems. Even Cindy Peterson. He might not be happy about her complaint to his boss, but when she'd told him at the Orchid on Friday night she'd make sure her son didn't trespass again, he knew she'd meant it. Although her negligence had caused the problem to begin with, she took responsibility for fixing things. Devon could learn a lesson or two from her.

"Sorry, sis. Not this time."

Dead silence stretched between them.

He waited her out.

"I only need a few bucks."

"What's a few?"

"Two hundred. I'm short for my portion of the rent."

"Why don't you pick up some extra waitressing hours?"

"I told you why." There was an edge to her voice now.

Scott stopped a few feet from the excavator, held up one finger to the operator and angled away, his own temper flaring. "I have a lot of expenses, too. Seaside Gardens costs a fortune. In fact, I wouldn't mind some help with those bills. Maybe you ought to think about getting a real job so you could contribute toward Gram's care."

"Man. Did you get up on the wrong side of the bed or what?" Irritation nipped at her words.

"Life isn't a picnic out here, Devon."

"Yeah? Well, it isn't here either. This business is cutthroat. But I'm on the verge of making it big with this new play, and I'm not going to blow my chance. Keep your money. I can always go to a homeless shelter if I can't come up with my share of the rent." The line went dead.

A muscle clenched in Scott's jaw as he jammed the phone back into the holster on his belt. Not even nine o'clock yet, and he was already down two strikes.

As he turned toward the crew awaiting his instructions, Devon's parting shot echoed in his mind. A homeless shelter. Like she'd ever follow through on that threat. What a dumb ploy.

But even dumber than that, he knew he'd end up wiring his sister the money before the day was over.

Just in case.

"Mom…it's that man from The Point!"

At her son's urgent tug on her sleeve, Cindy

stopped reading the label on the can she'd pulled from the shelf at the Mercantile and looked toward the front door, where the jingling bell was announcing a new arrival.

Her gaze collided with Scott Walsh's.

She stifled a groan. The last thing she needed after her crazy busy Wednesday was another encounter with the ill-tempered construction company owner. And judging by the sudden narrowing of his eyes, he wasn't thrilled to see her either.

Or maybe he was mad all over again because his boss had passed on her complaint.

She quashed a sudden twinge of regret. She had more important things to worry about than Scott Walsh's ego.

Intending to ignore him, she turned her back and addressed her son, who remained fixated on his nemesis. "It's not polite to stare, Jarrod. Why don't you go pick out an ice cream bar from the freezer for dessert?"

"He's coming over here." Her son relayed the news in a panicked whisper as he edged closer.

Cindy's pulse took a leap, and she tightened her grip on the can.

"Excuse me." The familiar deep baritone resonated in her ears. At least his tone was cordial rather than angry. A hopeful change.

Clutching the can, Cindy rotated toward him.

She'd known he was tall the night he'd towered over their table at the Orchid, but his full height registered now as he stood across from her. At five-seven she wasn't short, but he had to top six feet by an inch or two at minimum.

"I'd like to apologize for my rudeness last Friday and introduce myself. Scott Walsh." The hint of a smile that seemed forced pulled at his lips as he extended his hand.

He was hating this. Cindy could read it in his eyes and the taut stretch of his mouth. This was not a man who liked to apologize. Yet he was doing it anyway. That earned him a few points.

After transferring the can to her left hand, she took his fingers in a firm grip. "Cindy Peterson. And my son, Jarrod." When the youngster resisted her attempt to tug him out from behind her, she gave up. "I'm sorry if my conversation with your boss caused any problems. I'd had a long, stressful day and said more than I should have. My mouth sometimes gets away from me."

Her candor appeared to take him off guard, but surprise quickly morphed to amusement that put an appealing spark in his dark green irises. "As you may have guessed from this red hair and my comments on Friday, I can empathize with that. Shall we call it even?"

"Let's."

Her purse slipped from her shoulder as Jarrod eased out a fraction, and when she grabbed for it she dropped the can. Scott bent to retrieve it, scanning the label on the all-purpose bug spray before handing it back.

"Insect problem?"

"Ants in the kitchen." She wrinkled her nose. "There was a whole parade of them last night. I have no idea where they came from."

"They can be insidious. I had the same problem in my grandmother's house last month." He checked out the shelves behind her, then reached past her shoulder and snagged a different can. "I used this. Worked like a charm."

"Sold." She twisted around to replace the other can and took the one he offered. His fingers were long and lean, she noted, as they brushed hers. And the calluses on his palm told her he wasn't the kind of boss who directed from the sidelines. An odd flutter skittered along her nerve endings, and she eased away, hugging the can to her chest. "Thanks for the advice."

"Thanks for the understanding." He tipped his head sideways to get a better look at her son. "Bye, Jarrod."

It took a prod with her elbow to elicit a mumbled reply from her son.

With a lift of his hand, he disappeared around the end of the aisle.

Jarrod stayed close while she finished her shopping, but by the time she approached the high, old-fashioned counter at the seventy-five-year-old store that was one of her favorite town landmarks, Scott was gone.

The owner's daughter greeted her as she approached, waving a small white bakery bag. "From Scott." Lindsey tapped the plastic dome beside the cash register, where her homemade cookies were always displayed. "Chocolate chip today. He said to enjoy them for dessert." She grinned, her brown eyes twinkling. "Looks like you two have made a new friend."

"More like a peace offering." Nevertheless, Cindy had to admit it was a nice gesture. "We had a little…run-in with him last week."

"With Scott?" Lindsey raised an eyebrow as she rang up and bagged Cindy's purchases. "I've only heard good things about him."

The bell over the door jingled, and Lindsey leaned sideways to check out the new arrival. A tall, mid-thirties, sandy-haired man dressed in a National Park Service uniform entered. "Hi, Clint. That garden edger you ordered is in. Give me a minute to finish up here and I'll get it from the back."

"No hurry. I need a few other things anyway." The man brushed the dust off his slacks as he strolled over to the counter, exchanging a greeting with Cindy and Jarrod as he inspected the dome. "Save me a couple of cookies, okay?"

"No problem." Lindsey bagged Cindy's purchases and eyed Clint. "Where've you been anyway? A dustbowl?"

The man grimaced. "A construction site. I stopped by The Point a few minutes ago with the contractor who's going to develop the interpretive trail in the public-use area Mattson set aside. It's a mess out there. But I have to say Mattson's people are being accommodating. I ran into Scott Walsh, the foreman. Very cooperative. Seems like a good guy. He even offered us additional resources if we need them." Still brushing himself off, he snagged a cookie and headed into the store.

Cindy watched him go. Interesting. Clint Nolan had been in town for a couple of years, and he generally kept to himself, living alone on the first floor of the two-family home he'd bought a mile out of town. He'd gotten involved in the Save The Point campaign Lindsey had spearheaded but in a quiet, behind-the-scenes kind of way, and he rarely offered opinions unless asked.

Yet he'd been forthcoming in his appraisal of Scott.

The man must have impressed him.

Lindsey had obviously come to the same conclusion. She nodded in the direction Clint had disappeared. "See what I mean? And Scott's always been pleasant in our encounters. An excellent neighbor, too. He happened to be passing by last week while I was out in the lot debating what to do about a flat tire. He pulled in and changed it even though I told him not to bother."

"I might have just met him on a bad day."

"That's possible." Lindsey handed Cindy the receipt. "We all have those." A shadow flitted over the other woman's eyes, reminding Cindy that lots of people had problems far more serious than hers.

"But there are also happy endings."

"Yeah. There are." The tension in Lindsey's features relaxed. "You keep that in mind, too."

The bell jingled again to admit another customer, and as Lindsey turned to greet him, Cindy gathered up her bags. After handing one to Jarrod to tote, she pushed through the door and crossed the gravel lot to her Honda.

As she loaded the groceries in the trunk, Jarrod extracted the white bag containing the cookies and peeked inside, his expression puzzled. "How come he did this, Mom?"

"I guess he was trying to be nice."

"He wasn't nice to us last week."

"You don't have to eat his cookies if you don't want to." Stifling a smile, she closed the trunk as he pondered that. Fat chance her son would pass up homemade cookies—no matter the source.

"I don't want to throw them away." He crimped the top of the bag in his fingers and maintained a firm grip on it.

"Guess you'll have to eat them then."

"Yeah." He followed her around the car and climbed in. "So do you still think that guy is mean?"

"Do you?"

"I dunno. He was nicer tonight." He snapped his seat belt in place. "But I guess it doesn't matter. We probably won't see him much anyway."

That was true. Scott had been on the job site since the project broke ground in January, and their paths had only just crossed. With her working more hours than ever, the odds of them meeting again were slim.

Yet as they drove home, Cindy found herself wishing they *would* meet. Which was odd.

And unfair to Steve.

Besieged by guilt, she struggled to find a logical explanation for her reaction. But the best one she could come up with—that she wanted to reassure herself she and Scott had smoothed out their rocky beginning—was lame.

The real explanation was simpler. And it was based on chemistry, not logic.

Like it or not, back in the store she'd felt a subtle zing of attraction for Scott Walsh.

And she didn't like it.

Because it was one more complication in a life that already had far too many.

Chapter Three

Scott swung into a parking space near the E.R. entrance at St. Joseph's Hospital, yanked the key out of the ignition and pushed open the door.

This was not how he'd intended to spend his Friday night.

Two steps out of the car he realized he hadn't tucked in the shirt he'd thrown on after taking the call from Seaside Gardens. After pocketing his keys, he shoved the tail into his jeans without breaking stride, double-checked the rest of his attire—and discovered he'd also forgotten his socks.

But as long as Gram was okay he could cope with missing footwear. She'd already broken one hip. Another fall could be fatal.

His stomach clenching, he strode inside as the E.R. doors whooshed open to admit him. He didn't waste any time at the intake desk, and in less than a minute he was being ushered back to a treatment room.

As he passed the central nursing station, he caught sight of Paul Butler and slowed his pace. He'd known that his fellow congregant from Good Shepherd Church was a doctor, but he'd forgotten he worked at St. Joseph's.

"I've been watching for you." The man came around from behind the desk, white coat flapping. He took Scott's hand in a firm clasp and answered his question before he could ask it. "Your grandmother is in X-ray, but my preliminary exam didn't indicate anything more than a few bruises. The assisted-living facilities don't take chances with falls, though. We see a lot of elderly patients who go back as soon as we check them out."

The knot of tension in Scott's stomach loosened. "That's good news." The words came out hoarse, and he cleared his throat.

"You can wait in the treatment room for her to come back if you like." The doctor indicated a room four doors down. "But depending on how backed up X-ray is, it could be a while. If you haven't had dinner, you have time to visit the cafeteria. Or there are vending machines in the hall near the waiting room."

"Thanks. I'll hang out in the treatment room for now."

"No problem. Flag one of us down if you have any questions."

As the doctor returned to the desk, Scott continued toward the room. From the threshold he eyed the single hard plastic chair in the corner, hoping it was more user-friendly than it looked.

It wasn't.

After sixty futile seconds of contortions as he attempted to find a comfortable position, he gave up, determined to ignore the protest of his weary body.

Ten minutes later, though, it was more difficult to ignore the rumble from his stomach. Lunch had been a long time ago. Eight hours, to be exact, according to his watch. If the call from Seaside Gardens had come in even fifteen minutes later, he'd already have scarfed down the frozen dinner he'd been ready to nuke. Should he run to the cafeteria after all? Visit the vending machines? But what if some news came back on Gram while he was gone?

No. He'd stick it out for a while.

But thirty minutes later, when the complaints from his stomach and the unforgiving contours of the plastic chair ganged up on him, he stood. Five minutes. That's all it should take to run to the vending machines and appease his hun-

ger. The walk would also get the blood flow-
ing again to the other complaining parts of his
anatomy.

As he left the confined space and headed for
the waiting area, he surveyed the other treatment rooms. Most of the doors were closed,
suggesting a busy night. One was partly open,
however, and he spared it a quick glance as he
passed. A young boy was hunched over in a
hard plastic chair in the corner, similar to the
one he'd vacated.

A young blond-haired boy.

With a familiar face.

Scott stopped. Frowned. Backed up.

His eyes hadn't lied.

It was Jarrod Peterson. And he looked scared
out of his mind, his gaze riveted on a scene
blocked from Scott's view by a drawn curtain.

Who was back there? The boy's mother? Father? Both?

He had his answer a moment later when a
nurse lifted the curtain to exit the treatment
room. Cindy Peterson lay covered with a sheet,
her eyes closed, her blond hair spilling around
her shoulders, a large gauze bandage taped to her
forehead.

For the second time that evening, Scott's
pulse took a leap.

Angling toward the main desk, he scanned the busy staff behind it for Paul.

The doctor caught sight of him as he approached. "Sorry for the delay. They're swamped in X-ray."

"No problem. I was on my way to get some food and I caught a glimpse of Cindy Peterson." He gestured toward the treatment room.

"Are you two friends?"

"We're…acquainted. What happened?"

Paul gave him an apologetic shrug. "Sorry. I can't discuss her case. But you're welcome to speak with her." The doors to the ambulance dock banged open behind them, and two paramedics entered wheeling a stretcher. "Gotta run."

As Paul went to meet the arriving patient, Scott debated his next move. Cindy wore a wedding ring, but there was no sign of her husband in the treatment room. Was she here alone? Should he offer assistance—or lay low and respect her privacy?

All at once the door to Cindy's room opened and Jarrod poked his head out. As if seeking… help? When he spotted Scott, his eyes widened and he darted back inside, closing the door behind him.

Decision made. If Cindy did need help, Jarrod was too spooked by his presence to venture into enemy territory. In any case, he was no doubt passing on the news of his discovery at this very moment.

Scott walked over to the room and knocked. "Ms. Peterson, it's Scott Walsh. May I come in?"

There was a brief murmur of subdued voices before Cindy responded. "Yes."

He pushed the door open and rounded the privacy curtain. Her eyes were open now. Against the pallor of her skin and the white tape affixing the gauze pad to her temple her irises were an even more startling blue than he remembered.

A sudden, unexpected urge to reach out and take her hand in a comforting clasp swept over him, and he retreated a step, jamming his fingers in the front pockets of his jeans. Jarrod had beat him to it anyway. The boy had a death-grip on his mom's hand—though it was clear Cindy was the one doing the comforting.

"I saw Jarrod as I passed the room. You look like you had a close encounter with a hard object." He phrased the comment as an observation rather than a question. A simple *yes* or *long story* would suffice if she preferred not to share the reason for her visit to the E.R.

But she gave him the details.

"I was cleaning out a clogged gutter and the ladder tilted. I fell, hit my head on the brick garden edging and blacked out for a few seconds. When I came to Jarrod was already calling 911." She gave her son a smile. "He's a handy guy to have around in an emergency. No serious damage, though. The doctor thinks I have a mild concussion at worst."

"That is, in fact, the official diagnosis." Paul entered and grinned at Scott. "I see you made yourself at home."

Cindy looked from one to the other. "You two know each other?"

"We go to the same church. The pastor roped us both into working on the Christmas tree lot last year, and we became well acquainted as we scraped sap off our hands." The doctor checked over his shoulder at the activity behind him. "We're putting all your paperwork together, along with instructions. Once all that's done, you'll be free to go. But give us a few minutes. The victims of a multiple-car accident are arriving as we speak. No more ladders for a while, okay?"

"Maybe forever." As the doctor flashed a final grin and exited, Cindy brushed the fine hair off Jarrod's forehead. "Hang in a little longer, okay, buddy?"

"Yeah."

"So what are you doing here?" Cindy shifted her focus to Scott.

He gave her a recap of Gram's situation. "But Paul thinks she's just bruised. I hope he's right. She's had a rough year and a half. My grandfather died, she fell and broke her hip and then she had to leave her home of almost fifty years and move into assisted living. I'm not sure how many more setbacks she can take."

Cindy's eyes softened in empathy. "That's a lot of trouble to deal with all at once."

"Yeah." He raked his fingers through his hair, considering his next move. He'd still seen no sign of a husband—and Cindy was in no condition to drive, even if her car was here instead of back in Starfish Bay. Might as well take the plunge. "Assuming Gram's okay, she'll go back to Seaside Gardens in their van. Do you need a ride home?"

Cindy's lips parted slightly and she blinked. "Um…thank you, but that's too much of an imposition. I can call a friend."

No mention of a husband. Now Scott was more curious than ever. He opened his mouth to ask a leading question. Closed it.

Don't push, Walsh. It's none of your business.

"Okay. I hope you have a speedy recovery."

"Likewise for your grandmother."

He started to leave. Paused. If he'd missed dinner, had Cindy and Jarrod lost out on a meal, too? The blow to the head had probably killed

Cindy's appetite, but if Jarrod hadn't eaten he must be starving.

Turning back toward the duo, he directed his question to Jarrod. "Have you had dinner?"

The boy shook his head.

"Me, neither. I'm about to track down the vending machines. Can I bring you back some peanut butter crackers or a candy bar?" He cast a rueful glance at Cindy. "I doubt they have anything more nutritious than that."

Jarrod bit his lower lip, clearly tempted, but in the end he declined. "No, thank you."

"Are you sure, honey? It could be a couple of hours before I can get you any food."

"I'm sure."

"It's kind of you to offer." Cindy smiled at him, and the warmth in her eyes was like a shaft of sunlight on a cold day, dissipating the chill of loneliness he'd begun to accept as his lot.

For some reason he suddenly found it difficult to breathe. "No problem. Take care." Lifting his hand, he exited.

Time to fill the empty place in his stomach.

Too bad there wasn't a vending machine that could fill the empty place in his heart.

"Don't even think about it, Lindsey. Stay put. Tomorrow morning is fine." Cindy pushed back her hair, struggling to maintain a calm, in-control tone. "I'll call later and let you know where we're staying. We'll be fine." Removing the cell phone from her ear, she pressed the end button.

"What's wrong, Mom?" Expression anxious, Jarrod closed the space between them and laid a hand on her knee as she sat on the edge of the gurney.

"The coast road is fogged in." Despite the pounding in her temple, she did her best to summon up a reassuring smile. "Looks like we'll be spending the night here at a motel. They'll probably have cable." That was one extravagance she'd cut from their budget at home—and it was sure to appeal to Jarrod.

"Yeah? That would be cool. When can we leave?"

"Give me a minute and we'll be all set." She pulled her son close and laid her cheek against his fine hair. How was she going to muster the energy to deal with the logistics of summoning a cab, finding a decent motel and arranging for some food for her son? The mere thought of dealing with all that overwhelmed her.

"Excuse me again…"

At the familiar voice Cindy lifted her head and found Scott once again at the door.

"My grandmother was just released. Bruises only, I'm thankful to report. But I discovered the fog when I went out to the parking lot. I gather the coast road is socked in. I didn't know what arrangements you made, but if the friend you called lives in Starfish Bay, I think you're stranded."

"I just found that out. There are plenty of motels around here, though." A tremor shook her words, and she wondered if she looked as wan as she felt.

Apparently so, judging by the twin crevices that appeared on Scott's brow.

He folded his arms and narrowed his eyes. "Given your head injury, it might be better to stay with friends."

"All my friends are in Starfish Bay." She tugged Jarrod closer and somehow managed a smile. "But I've got my best buddy with me. We'll be fine."

He watched her, as if waging an internal debate. "Look, I'm living at my grandmother's house now. It has three bedrooms, including one with twin beds. You're welcome to use it tonight. It would be more comfortable than a motel, and I've got a fridge full of food. I don't know about Jarrod, but I'm starving."

The man was inviting her to spend the night at his house.

Cindy took a few beats to digest that. The gesture was kind, but Scott was a stranger. She couldn't possibly spend the night in the home of a man she'd met a mere week ago.

Could she?

She ticked off what she knew about him. He owned a reputable company, or he wouldn't have been hired by Louis Mattson. She'd heard nothing but positive things about him from Lindsey and Genevieve. Even Clint Nolan had gone out of his way to comment favorably on him. He had a kind heart, or he wouldn't have spent his Friday night hanging out in an emergency room with his grandmother. Plus, he was a churchgoing man, according to the doctor.

Surely it would be safe to accept.

Wouldn't it?

As if reading her thoughts, Scott gave her a one-sided smile. "I don't blame you for being cautious. Who knows, I could be an ax murderer." His teasing wink dispelled any such notion. "I'll tell you what. Why don't I call my minister and let him put your mind at ease about my character?"

She was fading fast, and if the man was willing to let her talk to his pastor, she was willing to give him the benefit of the doubt.

"That won't be necessary. I accept. With gratitude." She felt Jarrod stiffen beside her, and she gave his shoulder a reassuring squeeze.

The other side of Scott's mouth tipped up.

"Then let's get this show on the road. Are you ready to leave?"

"Yes. I have my papers in hand." She held up the instructions the nurse had left with her. "But are you certain you don't want to spend the rest of the evening with your grandmother?"

"After all this excitement, she'll be asleep five minutes after she gets back. I'll call and check on her from the house, though. Once I explain the situation, she'll be pleased I offered to help you out. She's always believed that performing charitable acts is good for the soul. This will earn me some brownie points." He flashed her a quick grin, displaying a disarming dimple. "I'm parked near the door. Are you steady enough to walk, or should we get a wheelchair?"

"The nurse already asked that. I'm fine."

"Why don't you take our arms at least—" he gestured to Jarrod "—just to be safe?"

The wisdom of his suggestion was apparent the instant her feet hit the floor. The room seemed to shift slightly, and she tightened her hold, feeling his muscles bunch beneath her fingers.

"Okay?"

His one-word query was laced with concern, and she lifted her chin. At this proximity, she could see the fine lines at the corner of his eyes that spoke of both sun exposure and worry, as well as the appealing flecks of gold in the depths of his green eyes.

"Ms. Peterson?"

At his prompt, warmth crept over her cheeks. "I'm fine. And since we're taking advantage of your hospitality for the night, I think it's time we switch to first names."

"Fine by me." He urged her toward the door. "There are a couple of spare toothbrushes at the house. Do you want to pick up any other toiletries on the way?"

"No." What she wanted to do was lie down again. As soon as possible.

He seemed to read her mind. "Gram's house isn't far. In less than half an hour, you'll be set for the night."

"Sounds great."

He didn't talk much during the drive, and her throbbing head was grateful for the quiet.

Fifteen minutes after they left the E.R., Scott pulled into the driveway of a bungalow largely obscured by the fog that had made navigating even the lighted city streets a formidable challenge.

"Let's get you inside and settled." He shut off the car. "How does some soup sound?"

"Perfect." Her stomach was empty but queasy. Soup, however, she could manage.

"Coming up in five minutes." He rounded the car to help her out. Jarrod continued to stick close, and he shot the boy a grin. "Once we get your mom down for the night, we can rustle up some real grub. I know I have fries in the freezer—and chocolate cake for dessert. If that's okay." He checked with her.

"Fine. Jarrod loves fries—and chocolate. Right?" She nudged her son, who had apparently lost his voice.

"Yeah."

She sent Scott an apology with her eyes as he fitted his key in the door that led from the attached garage to the house.

He responded with a reassuring smile. "I don't mind a challenge."

Grateful for his understanding, she let him lead her through the kitchen and into the hall. She had only a fleeting impression of the house, but it appeared well-kept and decorated in an understated, contemporary style she wouldn't normally associate with an octogenarian. Nor did the colorful, impressionist watercolors on the walls fit the stereotypical image of a senior citizen's dwelling.

Scott stopped at a door halfway down the hall and reached in to flip the light. "This used to be my sister's room. Gram didn't change it much. I hope it's okay." He inspected the furnishings as he spoke. "I haven't been in here much since I moved back six months ago. It might be dusty."

The twin beds were covered with patterned throws in bright colors, and several autographed pictures of show business personalities were framed on the walls. It looked like a teenager's room.

"It's fine—and far better than a motel. Thank you."

"The bathroom's right across the hall. I'll put out some clean towels for you. While you get settled, I'll heat the soup. Chicken and rice okay?"

"My favorite. Except for the broccoli cheddar at the Orchid."

He smiled. "I second that." Without prolonging the conversation, he retreated to the hall and closed the door.

As it clicked shut, Jarrod stuck his hands in his pockets and gave her a disgusted look. "Are we really going to sleep here?"

"I see you found your voice. And yes, we are." She carefully lowered herself onto the side of the bed and closed her eyes. Bliss.

"I bet he doesn't even have cable."

A lecture hadn't been on her agenda for this evening, but neither did she want Scott's kindness repaid with surliness.

Opening her eyes, she patted the bed beside her. "Sit. We need to have a talk."

"About him?"

"Yes."

He shuffled over and plopped on the bed, setting off fireworks in her temple.

"Jarrod!" She gritted her teeth and braced herself on the mattress. "Bouncing hurts my head."

"I'm sorry, Mom." His tone was subdued. Contrite. Carefully scooting closer, he put his arm around her. "I'm glad you're okay. I was really scared when you fell." His breath hitched. "What would I do if something happened to you?"

The broken words twisted her heart, and her aggravation evaporated. She wanted to assure him he didn't have to worry. That she'd be around as long as he needed her. But she couldn't promise that. They both knew better.

"I'm fine now, honey. And remember, no matter what happens, God is always with us." She pressed her cheek against his fine blond hair. After tonight's trauma, her son needed reassurance, not scolding. If he still had an attitude about Scott tomorrow, she'd address the issue then. She could, however, lay the groundwork tonight. "And we have a lot of people who care about us. Mr. Walsh, for one. He did a very nice thing by inviting us to stay with him to-night. Like the good Samaritan. You remember that story from the Bible."

"Yeah." He scuffed his toe on the carpet.

"Will you do me a favor?"

"What?"

"Go out and eat some dinner. You haven't had anything since lunch, so I know you're hungry. And try to be nice to Mr. Walsh."

"What if he yells at me again?"

"I doubt that will happen."

"I think he's only being nice 'cause he feels bad about how mean he was to us in the beginning."

"There may be more to it than that."

"Like what?"

Like what, indeed?

She could remind him again that Scott was living the very faith she and Steve had tried to instill in him. That he was performing an act of charity, as he'd said. And that was true.

But she couldn't help wondering if part of his motivation was more personal. If he, too, had felt the attraction between them.

She hoped not.

Because romance was at the bottom of her priority list.

"Mom?"

She was saved from having to answer by

a soft knock on the door and a muffled call. "Room service."

"Come in." She started to rise as Scott pushed the door open with his shoulder, but he waved her back to the edge of the bed.

"Stay put." He carried in the soup and a cup of tea on a collapsible TV tray and placed it in front of her.

"I haven't seen one of these in years." She touched the edge of the tray. "My mom had a set of them."

"Gram's got all kinds of old stuff like this stashed in the basement and the attic." He gestured toward the bowl of soup and tea. "Would you like anything else?"

"This is plenty. Thank you."

With a nod, he turned to Jarrod. "Why don't you stay with your mom while she eats? I'll raid the fridge and see what I can find for us."

"Okay."

"If you need anything tonight, Cindy, don't hesitate to let me know. My room's at the end of the hall."

Her gaze connected with his, and once more that electric jolt zipped through her. Based on the sudden darkening of his eyes and his abrupt step back, she suspected he'd felt the same thing.

"I'll be in the kitchen."

With that, he exited.

Leaving her to conclude that his invitation had, indeed, been prompted by more than charity—and to wonder if she'd made a big mistake by accepting.

Unfortunately, it was too late for second thoughts.

Chapter Four

Footsteps alerted Scott to Jarrod's approach, and he looked toward the hall as the boy entered carefully balancing the TV tray, eyes downcast. After setting it against the wall, Jarrod retreated to the doorway and hovered there, hands stuck in pockets.

Boy, did he have a lot of ground to make up with this kid.

Scott summoned up a smile, shut the door to the freezer section of the fridge and hefted a bag of frozen fries. "Found them. How's your mom doing?"

"She fell asleep. I was going to go to bed, too…but she made me promise to come out and eat."

In other words, he'd rather have gone hungry than share a table with the mean guy who'd scared him at The Point.

Scott had no regrets about confronting him that day. Better he be scared than injured. Or dead. But he did regret using his typical intimidation approach. There was an echo of sadness in Jarrod's eyes, as there was in Cindy's. Because the dad was nowhere to be seen, his guess was that a recent divorce had torn the family apart. And like any breakup, it had left victims in his wake.

Especially vulnerable children.

An image of seven-year-old Leah, with her long dark hair and big brown eyes, surfaced, and he clenched his teeth. He'd felt badly about ending things with Angela, but it was the memory of her daughter's stricken face the night he'd told her he wouldn't be coming around anymore that plagued him. He'd felt like a heel as the tears trailed down her cheeks. Worse still after she'd run from the room screaming that she hated him.

That was the moment he'd resolved never again to get involved with a woman who had children.

But tonight wasn't the time to dwell on regrets. He had a more pressing task—smoothing things out with Cindy's son.

"So do fries, burgers, corn on the cob and chocolate cake sound okay?" He tossed the package of fries onto Gram's speckled Formica counter and flipped the toaster oven setting to broil.

"Yeah. I guess." Jarrod remained in the doorway, as if poised to flee.

Scott propped his hip against the edge of the counter. "Will you come in if I promise not to bite? Scout's honor?" He grinned and held up his hand in a pledge.

The boy's face remained solemn. "Do you have cable?"

"No. Sorry." One more thing he'd given up when money got tight.

"I didn't think so." Letting out a resigned sigh, Jarrod shuffled into the room and slid into a chair on the other side of the table. As far from Scott as possible.

"Would you like some soda?"

Jarrod bit his lip. "Mom only lets me have soda on special occasions."

"The first visit to someone's house is a special occasion in my book." Cindy might not approve, but breaking a few rules might be the only way to loosen up her son.

"Yeah?" Jarrod brightened a few watts. "What kind do you have?"

"Check out the door." Scott gestured to the fridge.

The boy considered that. Taking inventory of the soda would put him close to his host. Scott could almost hear the wheels turning as Jarrod debated the pros and cons.

The pros won. He sidled over to the fridge and pulled open the door, keeping one eye on Scott as he selected a Sprite.

"My favorite, too." Scott handed him the bag of fries after Jarrod popped the tab on the can. "There's a baking sheet in the cabinet under the stove. Why don't you shake some of these onto it?"

He took the bag in silence and did as Scott asked. When he finished, Scott had him dig the frozen corn on the cob out of the freezer. In between he tried to engage the boy in conversation, but none of the subjects he introduced—sports, school, his recent spring break—broke the ice.

In the end, it was the scratching on the back door that did the trick.

Jarrod froze as he searched for a pot in the cabinet Scott had pointed out to him. "What's that?"

"Toby." Scott finished flipping the burgers. "Do you like dogs?"

"Yeah."

"Then you'll like Toby." He walked to the back door and opened it. "He's my grandmother's dog. Mostly he stays outside, but he likes to join me for dinner."

The white ball of fur bounded in the instant the door opened, tail wagging, eager eyes searching the room. He skidded to a stop after he spied Jarrod, front paws down, rump in the air. For a few seconds he checked out the interloper. Then his tail started a slow wag.

"Huh." Scott put the hamburger buns on plates as he watched Toby. "That's a first."

"What do you mean?" Jarrod and the dog continued to assess each other.

"He always expects to find Gram in the kitchen, and once he realizes she's not here, his tail usually droops and he just lays there whining. He still misses her a lot, even after almost a year."

"Can I pet him?"

"Sure."

Jarrod approached the dog, knelt beside him and stroked his fur. "What is he?"

"A mutt. Gram and Gramp got him at the pound about eight years ago. I think he's part cocker spaniel, but on the small side."

The dog inched closer to Jarrod and put his chin on the boy's knee. "He's nice." Jarrod continued to pet him as he spoke. "We had a great dog once, a little bigger than Toby. Her name was Skippy, and she was golden-colored. She was a mutt, too, but she was smart. I taught her to fetch and play ball." He leaned close and buried his face in Toby's fur. "She got hit by a car right after Christmas a year ago. Almost the same time my dad died."

The final, muffled words were a mere whisper—and laced with tears. But Scott had no difficulty hearing them.

Closing his eyes, he gripped the edge of the counter. Cindy was a widow, and Jarrod had lost his dad and his dog within weeks of each other.

No wonder they both looked sad.

In silence, he crossed to the boy and dog and dropped down beside them. Jarrod's shoulders were shaking, and Toby wiggled closer to him, as if sensing his new friend needed comforting.

"I'm sorry, Jarrod." He wanted to touch the boy but had a feeling the youngster would prefer Toby's ministrations. "It's really hard to lose people you love. I know. It happened to me, too."

Jarrod raised his head and swiped his sleeve across his eyes. "Your dad died, too?"

"Yeah. Also my mom. They were killed in a car accident when I was nine."

"Wow. That would be even worse." He sniffled. "I miss my dad a lot. Did you miss your mom and dad a whole bunch?"

The similarity in their stories ended with

their loss, but he wasn't about to tell that to Jarrod. So he sidestepped the question. "It's natural to miss people who have been an important part of your life. I was lucky, though. I had a grandma and grandpa who loved me. They brought me and my sister out here to live with them, and that helped a lot."

"Yeah. Like I have Mom. She takes real good care of me." Jarrod cuddled the dog closer, and Toby lifted his head to slurp the boy's cheek. "But what if…if something happens to her, too? What if she falls off another ladder? Or gets hit by a car? Or has a heart attack, like my dad?"

Heart attack. Scott filed away that new piece of information.

"Your mom's awfully young to have a heart attack."

"So was my dad."

Ah. Now he understood why Jarrod had looked terrified in the E.R. When you were eleven, the death of your remaining parent would wreak havoc in your life.

Given his recent losses, Scott had a feeling the trauma of this night would remain with the youngster for a long time and leave him worrying about stuff kids his age weren't supposed to worry about.

There wasn't much he could do to fix that

problem in the long-term, but maybe for tonight he could feed the boy a decent meal and keep him from fretting.

"Well, if you ask me, your mom looks very healthy—except for that bump on her forehead. I don't think you need to worry too much about anything happening to her anytime soon. You want to give Toby his dinner while I rustle up our burgers?"

"Sure."

"His food's in the pantry—" Scott rose and gestured to the other side of the room "—and his bowls are in the corner. Looks like he needs a refill on water, too."

As the boy took care of the dog, Scott served up their food. While Toby chomped through his own dinner in the corner, they took their seats.

"Do you and your mom usually say a blessing before you eat?"

"Most of the time."

"I do, too. I'll start, and you can add something at the end if you like."

Scott bowed his head and folded his hands. "Lord, we thank You for this food. We thank You for protecting Jarrod's mom from more serious injury, and we ask for her quick recovery. I also thank You for keeping Gram safe tonight, and I pray that You heal her body and spirit so she can come home again." He stopped, giving Jarrod the floor.

The youngster scrunched up his face. "Thank you for giving us a place to stay tonight. Please make Mom better real fast and make her job easier so she doesn't have to work so hard and worry so much. Please say hi to Dad for me, and would You tell him I still miss him? Amen."

Scott's throat tightened as he echoed the amen. The more he learned about the mother-son duo, the more guilty he felt about the distress he'd caused.

And what was Cindy's job, that it kept her too busy—and stressed?

As Scott passed the corn to Jarrod, he tried to think of a way to get more information without pumping her son. Nothing came to mind. At least nothing that wouldn't leave him feeling more guilty.

Jarrod was shoving fries into this mouth so fast Scott was afraid he was going to choke, and he moved the boy's glass of soda closer to his plate. "You might want to wash a few of those down before you create a logjam." He smiled, hoping that would soften the remark from criticism to suggestion.

In silence, Jarrod reached for the glass and took a long swallow. "These are good."

"I agree." Scott squirted some more ketchup

on his plate and swirled a fry in it. "They're not real healthy, but I have to confess I eat more of them than I should. Especially at the Orchid. They make the best fries I've ever had."

"Yeah. Mom and I eat there a lot, since she started working again. More in the last couple of months, 'cause she gets home later now. It's really busy at her job. Somebody quit, and everybody had to do more work. Now somebody else quit and they gave Mom her job. So she'll be even busier."

The perfect opening. It wasn't prying if you were responding to a comment.

Scott took a sip of his own soda. "What does she do?"

"She works for a museum here in Eureka. Doing history stuff. She likes it a lot most of the time, but she worries about leaving me alone after school, even though I'm almost twelve. I guess she's afraid I'll get into trouble. Like I did last week." The boy's voice grew more subdued and he broke eye contact to play with a fry.

"The Point is a dangerous place. Your mom is right to worry. But I'm sure you promised her you wouldn't go back there again."

"Yeah."

Toby finished his dinner and trotted over to see what he could scavenge from the table. He stopped at Jarrod's chair and placed one paw on the boy's leg. Scott stifled a grin. Smart dog. He knew better than to approach his caretaker.

Jarrod looked over at him. "I think he's still hungry."

Not likely. However, the dog knew how to use his soulful baby browns to advantage.

"I never feed him from the table. This kind of food isn't healthy for him."

"We had the same rule for Skippy. Sorry, Toby." Jarrod sighed and patted the white head.

Scott looked from boy to dog. Both of them could use a friend, and this was a surefire way to solidify the bond already forming between them.

Knowing he'd live to regret his decision, he relented. "Maybe we could break the rule once. With one fry."

"For real?" Jarrod's face lit up.

"Yeah."

"Cool!" He selected the biggest fry from his plate and held it down to the dog. "Here you go, boy. A special treat."

Toby gobbled it down in two long gulps, tail thumping. Then he lay beside Jarrod's chair and gazed up at him adoringly.

Mission accomplished.

They finished their meal on a more pleasant note, and Jarrod even offered to help load the dishwasher. By the time they put Toby out for the night and Scott walked him to his room, the boy was as relaxed as he'd ever seen him.

"Remember, if you or your mom need anything tonight, I'm right there." He pointed to the next door down on the same side.

"Okay. Thanks for dinner."

"You're welcome." He cracked open the door enough for Jarrod to slip through.

Soft light from the hall spilled in, faintly illuminating Cindy's sleeping form. She was on her side, facing the door, pillow scrunched under her head. In repose, her face was serene. Lovely. Appealing.

Too appealing.

He swallowed. When he'd issued his invitation earlier, he'd told himself it was the Christian thing to do. That there was no ulterior motive.

That had been a lie.

Cindy Peterson was a beautiful woman, and the temptation to get to know her better had been too strong to resist.

But that was a bad idea.

Breaking a rule about a dog was one thing.

Breaking a rule that could break hearts was another.

He wasn't going there again.

Stepping back to block her from his line of

sight, he managed to coax his lips into a smile. "See you in the morning."

And after shutting the door behind the little boy, he walked down the hall to his room. Alone. As always.

Despite a reluctance to rouse herself from the best sleep she'd had in months, Cindy couldn't resist the mouthwatering aroma of frying bacon that was tickling her nose.

Resigned, she lifted her eyelids—and found herself staring at a huge poster of George Clooney.

She blinked. Okay. Right. She was in Scott Walsh's sister's room in his grandmother's house. And the dull ache in her temple was the result of the mild concussion from her adventure on a shaky ladder last night.

Gingerly, she turned her head toward the other twin bed in the room. Empty. The bacon aroma had already gotten to Jarrod. She smiled at his attempt to make the bed. The pillow was crooked and the comforter hung too long on this side, reminding her of his bed at home. But he'd tried. That was the important thing.

Throwing back the covers, she swung her feet to the floor, gave her equilibrium a few seconds to adjust, then stood. The floor remained solid. A positive sign—as was the rumble in her stomach.

Time to check out that bacon.

Ten minutes later, after freshening up as best she could, she walked down the short hall toward the kitchen. The muted sound of voices—one deep, one higher-pitched—were too indistinct for her to make out the conversation, but a sudden laugh from her son sent a clear message. He and Scott had mended their fences.

Another positive sign.

When she reached the threshold, she found the two men in the house focused on a white, furry dog that sat next to the table beside Jarrod. The pup was quivering with eagerness, his head tipped back as he watched her son select a piece of bacon from his plate.

"You know, Toby will be spoiled rotten by the time you and your mom go home." Scott was standing beside the coffeepot, angled away from her as he filled the mug in his hand, his complaint mitigated by his good-natured tone.

"But you didn't feed him. He won't expect you to break the rule. Only me." Jarrod held out the bacon to the dog. He wolfed it down and nuzzled her son's knee. Jarrod petted him and turned his attention back to his plate, downing the last slice of his bacon as he slanted a look at Scott. "I guess he'd be happy if I came back to visit."

Cindy didn't miss the touch of hope in her son's voice. Talk about a change of heart.

She waited for Scott to respond, but as the silence lengthened she realized he didn't want to commit to any future invitations.

Stifling a surprising pang of disappointment, she came to his rescue. He'd already done far more than most people would have by taking them in last night. And his reluctance to make promises about any further contact quelled her concerns about sending the wrong message in case the attraction was mutual. Obviously it wasn't, or he'd have been all over Jarrod's comment. Besides, a man like Scott Walsh wouldn't lack for female companionship. For all she knew, he had a serious girlfriend. Better still, right?

Then why did she suddenly feel depressed?

"Mom!" Jarrod spotted her and jumped out of his chair to fly across the room. Skidding to a stop mere inches away, he toned down his exuberance and gave her a careful hug.

"Good morning." She kissed his forehead and sized up the two empty plates on the table. "I see you both got a head start on breakfast."

"We saved you plenty." Scott gestured to a

chair. "Have a seat and I'll dish it up. I hope you're hungry."

"Starved."

He remained by the chair until she took her seat, then slid it under the table. "See? I'm not always rude. Only when my temper short circuits the good manners my grandparents taught me." He smiled, displaying that endearing dimple in the corner of his cheek again. "And I try not to let that happen too often."

The man definitely knew how to turn on the charm.

She cleared her throat, shook out the napkin beside her knife—and tried to think of some witty response.

Her mind went blank.

"Hey, Mr. Walsh, I think Toby wants to go out."

Saved by the boy!

Toby had trotted over to the back door and stood patiently waiting.

"You're right." Scott moved away, leaving the faint trace of an appealing aftershave in the air. "If it's okay with your mom, you can go out with him." He addressed her as he unlocked the door. "Gram has a fenced yard. It's safe."

"Okay."

"Great!" Jarrod bounded out after the dog.

"So much energy at such an early hour." Scott

grinned as he closed the door and crossed to the oven to remove a foil-covered plate, grabbing a pot holder en route. "Would you like orange juice or coffee, or both?"

"Both, thanks, if it's not too much trouble."

He slid the plate in front of her. "Coffee's made, and I always have orange juice on hand." He loosened the foil and pulled it off, steadying the plate with his left hand.

His badly scarred left hand.

She stared at the network of shiny white lines. Why had she never noticed them before? And what sort of injury would cause that kind of scarring?

Before she could compose herself, Scott tugged off the paper and tucked his left hand in his pocket. Sending a clear message.

Not open for discussion.

Okay. Despite her curiosity, she didn't intend to invade his turf any more than she already had.

"Wow." Cindy focused on the plate brimming with bacon, hash browns, sausage and scrambled eggs, forcing herself to switch gears. "This is a feast. Almost like eating at the Orchid."

"Trust me. I'm no competition for the sisters. And Genevieve's cinnamon rolls are the icing on the cake. Pardon the pun." He retrieved the juice from the fridge, filled a mug with coffee and placed both in front of her. One at a time. With his right hand. "Cream or sugar?"

"Neither. I take it straight."

"A woman after my own heart." He settled into the seat across from her with his own java and inspected her forehead. "That's quite a bump."

She shrugged and dug into the eggs. "It looks worse than it feels." That was an understatement. After she'd peeled back the tape and removed the gauze this morning, she'd been shocked by the size of the black-and-blue goose egg with the scraped-raw center. "If it's too unappetizing, I can put the bandage back on."

"I already ate. How did you sleep?"

"Better than I expected." She continued to shovel in the food. When had she last been this hungry? She couldn't remember. "How's your grandmother this morning?"

"Bruised. Sore. Cranky. I'll stop by to see her later." He wrapped his fingers around his mug and studied the dark depths of his coffee, his expression troubled.

Cindy didn't want to pry. Not after the signal he'd sent about his hand. Yet neither did she want to appear uncaring. It was a fine line to walk, and she stepped along it with care. "From what you said last night, she's had more than her share of problems."

"Yeah. She's always been a strong person, but everyone has their limits. Even though the doctors all say she could come home again if she'd commit to some rigorous therapy, she doesn't believe it. Or doesn't choose to believe it. She's decided she's going to end her days at Seaside Gardens, and the sooner the better. She doesn't even ask about Toby anymore. It's as if she's already said goodbye in her mind. Once Gramp died, a lot of the spirit went out of her."

Cindy played with her hash browns. "That can happen. I lost my husband fifteen months ago. I know what she's going through."

"Jarrod mentioned that. I'm sorry. He said it was a heart attack?"

Her son had talked about his father to a stranger? That was a rarity. The two of them must have really clicked.

"Yes. He was an international business consultant. It happened on an overseas flight. The captain made an emergency landing as soon as he reached land, but Steve was already gone." Cindy took a sip of her juice, her hand steadier than she expected. "Jarrod had a tough time for a while. I took him to counseling for months, but his grades continued to slip and he became very withdrawn. We finally got past that, but I'm afraid last night's events might bring back the bad dreams and clinginess. Me working longer hours isn't going to help either." She forked another bite of sausage, but her appetite had diminished.

"Jarrod mentioned that, too." Scott lifted his mug and leaned back in his chair. "Sounds like you have a busy job. He said it was a museum of some sort?"

"The Humboldt County Historical Society. I went back to work about a year ago. I used to work at a museum in Dallas, but I quit after Jarrod was born. Steve and I agreed that a parent should be a child's primary caregiver if at all possible. A few years later we moved to Starfish Bay, where his parents lived, because we thought it would be a better environment in which to raise a child. And Steve's work was portable."

"Admirable choices."

Some nuance in Scott's inflection intrigued her, but when he offered nothing more, she continued.

"Anyway, not only are we shorthanded at the museum, I was also just promoted. It's a nice bump in salary, but now I've got three weeks to come up with a blockbuster theme for the centerpiece exhibit that kicks off the society's annual fundraising drive. I have no idea how I'm going to manage that." She took a deep breath and finished off the last sausage. After Scott's effort to prepare a nice breakfast, she wasn't going to insult him by leaving any of it. "But we were talking about your grandmother. Is there some hobby or interest that might tempt her to reinvest in life?"

"She used to love to paint." He gestured toward the living room. "All the impressionist-style pieces in the house are hers, but she gave that up after Gramp died, long before she broke her hip. She used to love Toby, too, and I even took him to see her once, in the garden where pets are allowed. I hoped that would give her an incentive to get well, but I think it had the opposite effect. She told me not to bring him anymore." His eyes clouded briefly, then cleared as he gave her a smile that seemed forced. "On a brighter note, the fog's lifted. I'd be glad to take you back to Starfish Bay."

"We've already overstepped the bounds of hospitality. I called a friend last night after we got here and arranged for a ride home. But thank you." She checked her watch and stood, fingertips pressed to the polished pine to steady herself. "I'd better round up Jarrod."

"I'll take care of it." He crossed to the back door, pulled it open and called out to her son.

Ten seconds later Jarrod zoomed inside. "Are we leaving, Mom?"

"In a few minutes. Let's go make sure we haven't let anything in the bedroom, okay?"

"Okay." He turned toward their host. "Thanks for letting me play with Toby. And for dinner. And breakfast."

"It was my pleasure." Scott's gaze connected with hers as he responded to her son.

Once again, something electric zipped between them.

And unless she was way off base, he felt it, too.

But Scott seemed reluctant to acknowledge it. And that was for the best. She had enough to deal with already. She didn't need to add the stress of a new relationship—or the guilt. How could she be having these feelings when she was barely past the traditional one-year mourning period?

It was best to just walk away with a thank-you.

Even if her heart said otherwise.

Chapter Five

Scott paused outside the door to Gram's room, adjusted one of the pink carnations in the vase of flowers he'd picked up en route to Seaside Gardens, then stepped inside.

For one fleeting instant her eyes brightened. Then she gave him a stern look. "Why are you wasting your money on flowers for an old woman?"

"Brightening someone's day is never a waste of money." He set the vase on the nightstand and gave her a once-over. "You don't look much the worse for wear."

"You should see the bruise on my leg."

"The doctor said it shouldn't keep you from getting your exercise. Let's walk."

"Forget it."

"Gram, you need to walk. If you don't use it, you'll lose it."

"Don't quote silly sayings to me. I'm too old for intimidation tactics."

"Okay." He sat in the cushioned chair against the wall and crossed an ankle over a knee.

She gave him a wary look. "Aren't you going to badger me like you usually do?"

"Nope. I'm too tired today. I had company last night, remember?"

"Of course I remember. I have a bad hip, not a bad brain. Did your guests keep you awake?"

As a matter of fact, they had. Or one of them had. The one with blue eyes, sleeping on the other side of the wall. All through the long dark hours, he'd kept picturing her blond hair spilling across the pillow, the way it had looked when he'd glimpsed her before he and Jarrod had parted for the night. He doubted he'd clocked more than three hours of shut-eye.

"My guests were fine. I just didn't sleep well."

"So tell me what happened. You were very cryptic on the phone."

He gave her the short version, sticking to the basics, hoping she wouldn't try to read too much between the lines, as she often did.

No such luck. Her eyes grew more and more animated as he talked.

"This widow is the same woman you met

a week ago, with the trespassing son? Is she pretty?"

"She's attractive." He did his best to maintain an impassive expression as he delivered that understatement.

"How old is she?"

"I didn't ask."

"No, of course not. That would be rude, and I raised you to be polite. Let's see, if she has an eleven-year-old, she's probably about mid-thirties. That's a perfect age."

For you.

Gram didn't say that, but he could read between the lines, too.

When he didn't respond, she adjusted the blanket and laced her fingers on top. "Is she nice?"

"We had a pleasant conversation."

She narrowed her eyes. "Is that all you're going to tell me?"

"There's nothing more to tell."

"Hmm. You just don't want me jumping to conclusions, do you?"

"There aren't any conclusions to jump to. A very nice-looking man picked her and her son up this morning. It was clear the three of them knew each other well—and liked each other a lot."

Gram's face fell. "Was he her boyfriend?"

"That's my assumption. But she introduced him simply as a friend."

"Well, there you are." She jabbed a finger his direction. "I think *you're* the one jumping to conclusions."

"I don't think so." Cindy's smile had been warm as she'd greeted the man, and Jarrod had launched himself at the guy. It had all been very, very cozy.

And surprisingly, he'd experienced an odd twinge when he'd opened the door to admit the man. It had almost felt like…jealousy.

How nuts was that? He'd known Cindy for less than a week. And even if he was interested, she was a woman with a child. All he had to do was picture Leah's face to shore up his determination to avoid repeating that mistake.

"Scott, are you still with me?"

At Gram's question he refocused. "Yeah. I'm with you, but it doesn't matter what conclusions either of us jump to. I'm not interested."

"Why not?"

"Gram, let it go. Jarrod gave Toby quite a workout, by the way."

The brightness in her eyes dimmed, and she settled back on her pillow. "I don't want to talk about Toby. And you're changing the subject."

"That's right."

"Maybe I'll walk if you tell me some more about this nice lady and her son."

Despite her age, Gram hadn't lost one iota of her shrewdness. She'd thrown out the one bargaining chip she'd known he couldn't resist.

"Fine." He stood and retrieved her walker, positioning it beside the bed. "But we're going up and down the hall twice."

"My leg hurts." She clamped her lips together and folded her arms.

"Twice. I checked with your doctor. He said that was no problem. In fact, he encouraged it."

She held her ground for a few moments, then huffed out a sigh. "Oh, all right. You win. But you better make this worth my while."

He stifled a groan. Nothing short of an engagement announcement would satisfy Gram. She'd been after him for years to get married.

But it wasn't happening with the attractive widow. Cindy and Jarrod had already suffered more than their share of hurt and loss, and with two vulnerable hearts involved, pursuing a relationship was too risky.

No matter how potent the chemistry was between him and the lovely widow.

"What're you doing, Mom?"

As Jarrod dropped into the chair beside her at the kitchen table, Cindy licked the flap on the envelope and pressed it closed with her thumb. "Writing a thank-you note to Mr. Walsh. Did you finish all your homework?"

"Yeah." He planted his elbow on the table and cupped his chin in his palm. "You know, it wasn't so bad staying at his house. I liked Toby a lot. Do you think I'll ever get to see him again?"

Based on Scott's reaction to Jarrod's broad hint yesterday, not likely. But better to let her son down easy.

"I don't know, honey. Mr. Walsh is a busy man."

"I guess." He expelled a resigned breath and leaned back.

"You never did tell me what you had for dinner."

"French fries, burgers, corn, chocolate cake. He's got a lot of food in his freezer. Mostly microwave dinners. But not very much in the refrigerator part. I guess he eats frozen stuff 'cause it's easy to fix. The dinner was okay, but I like your food better. You cook real good."

"Thanks, honey." Cindy fingered the note, thinking about Scott's stockpile of frozen entrees. A simple note seemed such a paltry gesture in light of all he'd done for them. Not many people would welcome two virtual strangers into their home—and entertain a youngster, to boot.

Should she invite Scott to dinner? No doubt he'd appreciate a home-cooked meal.

A tingle ran up her spine at the thought of Scott sharing her table—and that made her decision easy.

No way. Asking the man into her home would be asking for trouble.

Jarrod wandered over to the sink to fill a glass with water. "Since we aren't going hiking in the redwoods, can I watch a movie?"

"Sure. And we'll get that hike in next week." Cindy had hated to cancel their afternoon plans. Sunday family outings were a tradition she and Steve had started, and although she'd let the habit lapse after he died, she'd resurrected it in the past few months.

However, while the pounding in her head had dulled, it was by no means gone. A tramp through the woods would have to wait. "I might even join you for part of the movie once I finish a few chores. Especially if you watch *The Adventures of Robin Hood.* It's hard to beat Errol Flynn."

A smile hovered at her lips as she recalled the movie nights the three of them had enjoyed as they'd watched a vintage film from Steve's DVD collection and shared a huge bowl of popcorn. Jarrod had loved those evenings.

"Okay. I like that one." He finished off his

water, set the glass on the counter and disappeared in the direction of the family room.

Before her melancholy thoughts could take hold, the doorbell rang. Odd. Who would come calling uninvited on a Sunday afternoon?

A quick check through the peephole brought her smile back, however. Lillian from the Orchid was standing on the other side, a wicker basket hooked over her arm, the contents covered with a checkered cloth.

The Starfish Bay version of meals-on-wheels.

Cindy opened the door. "This is a nice surprise. Come in."

"I'm not here to visit. I doubt you're up for that." Lillian leaned close to inspect the bump on Cindy's forehead. "My. That's a nasty one. Genevieve and I are on our way to the college for the arts festival. Janice is coming along to interpret the artwork for us." She flapped her hand toward the car, and the local gallery owner and Genevieve waved. "Then we're going to take in the play. We didn't think you'd be up to cooking, so here's something to tide you over until tomorrow." Lillian handed over the basket.

As Cindy took it, her eyes widened. "Wow. This feels like enough food for a week."

"Not at all. You just enjoy it. Wouldn't hurt you to put some meat on your bones."

As if the older woman could talk. While her

sister was short and a bit rounded, Lillian was tall and spare. There wasn't an ounce of fat on her lean frame. But Cindy refrained from pointing that out.

"Thank you. It seems Jarrod and I have been blessed with an abundance of generosity in the past twenty-four hours."

"Yes. I heard how Scott Walsh saved the day."

Even after seven years in Starfish Bay, Cindy was still surprised at how quickly news spread. "Let me guess. You stopped at the Mercantile."

"Otherwise known as news central. Lindsey hears everything." Lillian grinned, then touched her cropped dark hair, which sported only a few streaks of gray despite her seventy years. "I do believe I felt a raindrop. We'd best get on the road. You rest up and take care of yourself."

She hurried back to the car, and as they drove off Janice stuck her hand out the window and waved again.

Janice.

Now there was an idea. Pursing her lips, Cindy closed the door. Maybe the best—and safest—way she could thank Scott for his hospitality would be to try and lift his grandmother's spirits. It was obvious he was worried about her. She could send flowers, since she'd spent the night in the woman's house, but perhaps there was more she could do. Scott's grandmother was a talented painter. Janice liked to feature local artists. Could she pair the two of them up? Would that make Scott's grandmother take a new interest in life?

Back in the kitchen, Cindy deposited the basket on the counter as mouthwatering aromas drifted through the air. The sisters' rosemary pork tenderloin, she speculated, leaning closer to sniff. Far better than anything she'd have thrown together tonight.

But before she put the food away or joined Jarrod for the movie now well under way—based on the rollicking music coming from the family room—she was going to take a second stab at her thank-you note. And make a suggestion that would allow her to express her appreciation to the tall construction company owner in a much more concrete way.

"She wants to show my paintings to an art gallery owner?" Gram stared at Scott as if he'd suggested she take up Rollerblading.

"Why not? I think it's a great idea. I always said you had talent. This is the chance to show it to the world." He took her arm to steady her as they maneuvered around a corner and started back toward her room.

"I'm not good enough for that. How did this come up anyway?"

Scott tapped his shirt pocket. "I found a thank-you note from her in the mailbox tonight. She asked me to broach the subject with you."

Gram peered at him. "Sounds like an April Fool's Day joke to me. One day early."

"It's not a joke. She knows the gallery owner. I've met her, too. She's a very nice woman who likes to feature local artists."

"I'm not local."

"Close enough."

They arrived back at her room, and as she entered she released her grip on the walker to gesture toward an English-garden-in-a-vase bouquet that took up most of her nightstand. "I must admit I was bowled over by that. Your houseguest has good manners, I'll say that for her."

No argument there. Scott had been taken aback by the thoughtful gesture, too, when he'd arrived last night to visit Gram.

"You know, I wouldn't mind meeting her." Gram settled on the edge of her bed, the studied casualness of her tone putting him on alert.

His grandmother had her matchmaker hat back on.

"She's very busy." He helped her into bed, stowed the walker in the corner, then returned to adjust the covers. "What limited free time she has, she spends with her son."

"Sounds like she's a caring, conscientious mother."

"I'd say that's true, from what I've seen. What do you think about her idea?"

Gram squinted at him. "I don't know. I need to think about it."

"Fair enough. Is there anything I can do for you before I leave?"

"No. I'm well taken care of here." She patted his hand. "You're a good boy, Scott. Faithful. Loyal. Excellent husband material."

The woman had a one-track mind. "Not in the market."

"A pity. Well, go home and get some rest. And if you talk to Devon, tell her I expect a call. I haven't heard from that girl since she called to lament about her cash-flow problems a week ago. Have you?"

"Yes."

"Did she ask you for money?"

"Yes. I told her no."

Gram studied him. "But you sent it anyway."

Warmth crept up his neck as he shrugged.

"Hmph. That girl is going to have to learn to stand on her own two feet one of these days, you know."

"I know."

Once more she patted his hand. "You have a kind heart. Just like Cindy."

Leaning down, he kissed her on the forehead. "Good night, Gram."

"I'll think about the paintings. You think about finding yourself a wife."

"You're a hopeless romantic, you know that?"

She squeezed his hand. "No. Hope*ful*. Now go get some rest. And start putting some of your energy into finding a good woman instead of pouring it all into your work. I want you settled down before I go home to the Lord."

Scott let that pass.

Yet as he walked down the hall and left the building, Gram's advice echoed in his mind.

The problem was, he had a feeling he *had* found a good woman. To confirm that, though, he'd have to get more involved. Meaning, if it didn't work out, two more people would get hurt.

And he didn't want another Leah haunting his dreams.

"If it isn't our good Samaritan!"

As Genevieve beamed at him—and several other customers waiting to be seated at the Orchid looked his way—Scott felt a flush crawl up his neck. It was too much to hope that in a town the size of Starfish Bay a 911 call would go unnoticed. Half the residents had probably called to check on Cindy and then heard the whole story.

"It was no big deal, Genevieve. I had plenty of room."

"Doesn't matter. It was a very neighborly gesture. I know Cindy was most grateful. Are you here for takeout, or would you like to stay for dinner?"

"I'm staying tonight."

"Glad to hear it. It's not healthy to always eat on the run. I should have a table opening up in less than five minutes. Have a seat while you wait."

Scott wandered over to one of the chairs lined up against the wall and sat while Genevieve bustled about seating the customers who'd arrived before him. He ought to head back to the house. But it had been a long day, and the temptation to enjoy his evening meal in a homey place like the Orchid instead of in his silent kitchen with only a sulking Toby for company had been too hard to resist.

As he waited, Lindsey walked around the corner from the dining area. When she crossed to him, he rose.

"If you're staying for dinner, I can recommend the pot roast. It's amazing."

"Sold."

"How's Cindy doing? I haven't seen her since the accident."

He shifted his weight from one foot to the other. Lindsey's assumption that he was keeping tabs on his houseguest was more than a little unsettling.

Before he could respond, Nate Garrison rounded the corner, draped one arm over Lindsey's shoulders and held out his hand. "Nice to see you again."

The guy who'd picked up Cindy and Jarrod at his house was involved with Lindsey?

Distracted, Scott returned his firm grip.

"I'm glad you two had a chance to meet. I was planning to pick up Cindy and Jarrod Friday night until the fog socked us in. Nate filled in for me Saturday morning while I minded the store." Lindsey smiled up at the man. "Did you guys have a chance to get acquainted?"

"Not really." Nate dug his keys out of the pocket of his jeans. "Cindy and Jarrod were ready to leave when I arrived. How's she doing?"

"I'm not sure. I haven't…"

"Lindsey, is this yours?" Genevieve hurried over, holding a tube of lipstick aloft. "I found it on the seat of the booth."

The younger woman felt in the pocket of her slacks. "Yep. It must have slipped out. Thanks, Genevieve."

"Not a problem. Can't send you out into the world lipstick-less." She grinned and handed it over. "I've got a table for you now, Scott."

He said goodbye to Lindsey and Nate, watching them exit as Genevieve retrieved a menu.

"Nice couple." She rejoined him. "I'm a sucker for happy endings."

"So they're…involved?"

She chortled. "I'd say so. They're getting married next month in the tiny chapel you salvaged and reconstructed out on The Point. Why do you ask?"

Striving for a nonchalant tone, he lifted one shoulder. "Nate and Cindy and Jarrod all seemed very…friendly…on Saturday when he picked them up."

Her eyes twinkled. "They are. Nate and Lindsey tutored Jarrod when he fell behind in school after his dad died. Nate and Jarrod bonded, and Cindy is very grateful for all Nate did to help him get past his grief and move on."

She tucked the menu into the crook of her arm and gave him a keen look. "But in case you're wondering, there was never anything romantic between Nate and Cindy. He only has eyes for Lindsey. They were childhood friends, and once they reconnected last summer, it was clear to everyone but them that they belonged together. Fortunately, they saw the light, too.

Long story short—Cindy's unattached. And speaking of Cindy…" She glanced over his shoulder, toward the front door, and lifted her eyebrows.

Turning, he found his houseguest stepping into the foyer, a wicker basket over her arm.

She hesitated for a fraction of a second after she spotted him, then walked over. "Hi. This is a surprise."

Before he could return her greeting, Genevieve spoke up. "If Jarrod's with you, I have a nice table for three available. You could join Scott."

Genevieve was as bad as Gram.

A soft blush rose on Cindy's cheeks. "I only have time for a quick takeout. Parent-teacher meetings are tonight, and I'm already running late. Jarrod's in the car. I'll just take two of the specials. I also wanted to return this." She set the basket on the counter. "Thank you again for the meal. It was delicious—and much appreciated."

"Happy to do it." Genevieve picked up the basket. "You two can chat while I round up those dinners."

As the older woman took off toward the kitchen, Scott inspected the abrasion on Cindy's forehead. The bump was gone, a scab had formed over the scraped area and the bruise was beginning to fade. "That looks a lot better than it did the last time I saw it."

"It feels a lot better, too."

"You know, I'm glad I ran into you. I was planning to call tonight to thank you for the flowers you sent Gram and for your offer to show her paintings to Janice. I talked to her about it last night, and she's mulling it over. I consider it a positive sign that she didn't say no outright."

"I was hoping the idea might lift her spirits. I'll keep my fingers crossed. Has she recovered from her fall?"

"For the most part." Scott propped a hip against the end of the stool-lined counter that doubled as a check-in desk for the sisters' adjacent motel. "How's the exhibit project coming?"

Her face clouded. "It's not. I've been poring over books and artifacts, but nothing is generating any exciting ideas—and the clock is ticking."

"Here you go, Cindy." Genevieve pushed through the swinging door to the kitchen. "I told Tony to step on it. Can't have you late for a parent-teacher conference, especially when I expect you'll hear positive things this year. I don't know what Lillian and I would do without that man in the kitchen." She handed over a large white sack.

Cindy passed her credit card to the older woman, who fiddled with the manual credit card machine that shared space on the counter with an ancient cash register.

"Is Lillian still working on you about joining the computer age?" Cindy smiled at her.

"All the time." Genevieve gave a long-suffering sigh and handed Cindy the credit card slip for a signature. "This old brain isn't wired for all those electronic gizmos."

"Your brain is as sharp as anyone's I've ever met." Cindy wrote her name on the slip and handed it back. "Just take the plunge."

"Sound advice, I expect." She looked from Cindy to Scott and back again.

Cindy dipped her head and made a project out of rummaging in her purse for her keys. "I've got to run." She flashed Scott a quick look. "Let me know what your grandmother says."

"I'll do that." He walked with her to the front door and pulled it open as she exited.

"Thanks."

She paused for an instant to give him a smile, and he caught the hint of a subtle, fresh fragrance that evoked thoughts of flowers and spring. It was the same fragrance he'd noticed last Friday as he'd helped her to his car after they left the E.R. And the same one that still lingered in Devon's old room. He knew because he'd ducked in there more than once over the past week to inhale it.

Pretty pathetic.

He needed to get a life.

Turning back, he found Genevieve watching him with a smug smile. "Such a nice woman. Lovely, too, don't you think?"

"Very." He stepped away from the door and gestured toward the restaurant. "Now how about some of that pot roast? I'm starving."

"Coming right up." She led Scott toward his table, waiting as he slid into his seat. "Cindy told us why you were in the E.R. the night you ran into her. We're mighty sorry to hear about your grandmother's troubles. Once she's over her fall, you bring her up here for lunch or dinner someday. A change of scene can do a body a world of good."

Relieved she'd dropped the subject of Cindy, he considered the suggestion. "That might not be a bad idea. I haven't been able to tempt her to leave Seaside Gardens yet, but it doesn't hurt to try."

"Make it worth her while." She leaned close and winked. "Most people can be persuaded to step out of their comfort zones with the right incentive."

As she returned to the foyer to greet more

arriving customers, Scott took a long sip of his water. That last comment hadn't been only about Gram. Genevieve had donned her matchmaker hat again.

Scott didn't doubt the truth of the café owner's remark. Assuming Cindy felt the chemistry between them, he might be able to convince her to go out with him.

But that wouldn't be wise. What if he let things go on too long, made the same mistake again? He couldn't risk that.

Leaving two broken hearts behind was already two too many.

Chapter Six

Sitting back on his heels, Scott surveyed Gram's attic in dismay. Sorting through the detritus of his grandparent's life—and several other lives, he suspected, eyeing a couple of antique trunks—wasn't a job he relished. Especially on a Saturday morning. But she'd been insisting for weeks that it was time to sell the house, that she didn't want him spending any more of his money on her care. Nothing he'd said had dissuaded her.

With a sigh he picked his way over to a large, weathered trunk that had a rounded lid and reminded him of a treasure chest from a pirate ship.

Except he doubted it was going to contain a fortune in gold doubloons.

He gave it an experimental tug. It didn't budge. The thing was probably crammed with a bunch of decaying junk.

Pivoting toward the flat-topped wooden sea chest beside it, he dropped to the balls of his feet and gave it a slight push. Nada. It was just as heavy.

Resigned, he fiddled with the tarnished brass key stuck in the lock. After a couple of tries it turned, and he lifted the lid. A cloud of dust rose, and he backed off to wave it aside, waiting until it cleared before leaning in for a closer look.

The carved heart inside the lid caught his eye, and he squinted at the name inside. Emma. His great-great-grandmother. Interesting.

Yet it wasn't her trunk, based on the contents. On one side, a captain's hat rested atop a folded uniform coat that appeared to have escaped the notice of moths. He carefully lifted the edge of the wool jacket. Underneath was a collection of personal items—a worn Bible; straight razor; framed sepia portrait of a woman in a high-necked blouse and another of a couple in wedding finery; a small embroidered wall hanging that said, "At home I wait, your true first mate"; a bundle of letters tied with faded ribbon; a journal; several scrimshaw pieces; and lots of other odds and ends he didn't bother to sort through.

The other side of the chest contained tools of he seafaring trade, among them a mahogany-

and-ivory sextant, a ring of brass keys, what appeared to be a rudimentary first-aid kit, maps, a pistol and a logbook. Tucked in the bottom was a small tea chest.

Scott lifted the sextant, which appeared to be in perfect condition. This stuff must have belonged to Elijah Adams, his great-great-grandfather. Gramp had mentioned him a few times while he and Devon were growing up, but all he remembered was that the man had been in the U.S. Revenue Cutter Service in the late 1800s.

Switching his focus to the other chest, he lifted that lid and took a quick inventory. An old-fashioned satin-and-lace wedding gown rested on top, looking far more fragile than the uniform jacket in the first trunk. Scott didn't want to risk poking around too much for fear it would disintegrate, but he did peek underneath. He spotted a framed photo of a whiskered man wearing the cap in the first chest—surely Elijah—and a number of pieces of primitive art that looked as if they might have come from Alaska.

Scott closed the lid and sat back on his heels. Why had Gram never mentioned these artifacts? And when had they been put up here? He'd been in the attic on a few occasions during his younger years and the trunks hadn't been here then. He'd have noticed the pirate chest.

Even more intriguing—might this treasure trove possibly give Cindy an idea for her exhibit? Elijah and his wife had lived in Eureka.

Abandoning his plan to clean out the attic—for today, anyway—Scott pulled his cell phone from his belt and punched in Gram's number. She answered on the second ring.

"Morning, Gram. How are things today?"

"Same old, same old. The Lord hasn't taken me yet."

He ignored that comment and forged ahead. "I have a question for you. I'm checking out the attic like you asked, and I found two old chests up here. I think they belonged to my great-great-grandparents. The sea captain and his wife."

"Oh, my. I'd forgotten all about those. Yes, they did, and they'll be a bear to deal with. They're heavy as lead, as I recall. I had to pay those delivery people extra to haul them up to the attic and bribe them with my carrot cake. But it worked. They caved after I gave them a sample."

He believed it. Gram made a killer carrot cake. Or she used to. Man, what he wouldn't give for one more piece of it.

But that was a challenge for another day.

"Yeah, they weigh a ton. Where did they
me from?"

"Your father's aunt. She came across them when she was closing up her house to move into an apartment. She'd never married, so there were no children to pass them on to, and she thought someday you and Devon might want to have them. That was fifteen, twenty years ago. To be honest, I'd forgotten all about them. I never even looked inside."

The timing of their arrival explained why he'd never seen them. He must have been away at college when they'd shown up.

"Well, I opened them and they're packed with history." He sneezed and took another futile swipe at the dancing dust motes. "Remember I mentioned that Cindy Peterson works at the historical society? She's trying to come up with a theme for the big annual display that kicks off the fundraising drive, and this stuff might give her some ideas. Would you mind if I showed her the trunks?"

Silence.

"Gram?"

"I'm here. Just thinking."

Uh-oh.

"That might be okay, but I'd want to meet her before she goes poking around in our family history."

He knew where this was leading. "I could ask her to call you."

"You can't get to know anything about a person over the phone. Why don't you bring her over here and introduce us? Tomorrow, if she's available. I'd like to talk with her about showing my paintings to that friend of hers, too. We could kill two birds with one stone."

Three was more like it, counting Gram's matchmaking schemes.

Scott wasn't thrilled about subjecting Cindy to his grandmother's less-than-subtle efforts to get him hitched. But assuming Gram liked her—and how could she not?—his charming houseguest might have better luck than he'd had convincing Gram to show her paintings. And anything that could help lift her spirits was worth a few uncomfortable minutes.

Still, he made one more attempt to dissuade her.

"I'll give her a call, but she may already have plans for tomorrow. Besides, it would be easier for her to drop by and see you next week when she's in town. The historical society isn't far from Seaside Gardens."

"I want you to introduce us. Since you know her, you can keep the conversation going if it starts to lag."

No chance of that, not with Gram on a mission. But he wasn't going to win this battle.

"Fine. I'll let you know."

"I'm hanging up now so you can call her."

The line went dead.

Shaking his head, Scott slipped the phone back on his belt and descended the pull-down attic steps. At the bottom, he tugged on the rope to activate the spring that folded them back up into the ceiling. Then he called directory assistance. He'd keep his conversation with Cindy brief. No way did he want her to think this was some scheme he'd concocted just to see her again.

Although he had to admit he was more pleased by the prospect than he should be.

Cindy closed her car door, waited for Jarrod to get out, then pressed the autolock button as he shuffled around to her side, dragging his feet.

"Why did we have to come here anyway?" He inspected the grounds in front of Seaside Gardens, where several of the wheelchair-bound residents were soaking up some sun. "We could have hiked for another hour."

"I'm pooped. And I already told you why we're here. Scott's grandmother has some trunks in her attic full of artifacts that might help me with my exhibit." She wasn't about to pass up a chance to muster some ideas, even if her buoyant reaction to seeing Scott again had unsettled her.

"It's all old people here."

"So? Genevieve and Lillian are older, too, and they're a lot of fun."

"Yeah, but they're happy all the time. None of these people look happy."

She couldn't argue with that. Some of the residents were slumped, dozing in their chairs. Most of those who were awake wore glum expressions. The ones shuffling along with walkers, aides by their sides, seemed to be struggling or in pain or wishing they were anywhere but here.

No wonder Scott's grandmother's spirits were sagging. With all the trials she'd already faced, she needed to be in an uplifting environment, not one that was downright depressing.

"Cheer up." She patted Jarrod's shoulder and started toward the entrance. "We won't be here long."

As they approached the door, Scott stepped through. In all their previous encounters, he'd been wearing work clothes—jeans, cotton shirt rolled to the elbows, heavy boots. Today he'd exchanged the more casual attire for dark dress pants, black leather shoes polished to a military sheen and a white dress shirt with a thin green stripe that matched his eyes.

Wow.

In her worn jeans and T-shirt, she suddenly felt underdressed—and self-conscious.

"I've been watching for you." Scott smiled, checked his watch and held the door open for them. "I see punctuality is one of your virtues. How was the hiking?"

"Wonderful. It's hard to beat a day in the redwoods."

"True. What's your favorite trail?" He directed his question to Jarrod as the door closed behind them and he took the lead down a hall.

"Brown Creek."

"I like that one, too. Did you see any banana slugs?"

"Yeah. Four." Her son eyed Scott. "Do you like to hike?"

"When I have the time. Which hasn't been often lately. Prairie Creek is a great place."

"Me and my dad went there a lot."

Cindy dropped back a step as the two males chatted. For months after Steve's death, Jarrod had refused to go back to the state park where he'd spent so many happy hours with his father. Nate Garrison had finally convinced him to return, but her son still didn't talk about the place much with anyone else.

Interesting that he'd opened up to Scott.

When they reached a T in the hallway, Scott

stopped and gestured to the left. "It's the third door on the right."

She expected him to proceed, but instead he hesitated as if he was uncomfortable. "Is something wrong?"

"No. Maybe." He rubbed the back of his neck, then motioned toward a nurse's station a few yards away and spoke to Jarrod. "There's a bowl of Hershey's Kisses on the desk. If it's okay with your mom, you can take a few."

"Can I, Mom?" Jarrod gave her a hopeful look. "I'm starving."

Cindy picked up the cue. Scott wanted to talk to her alone. His ploy was obvious, even if the reason for it wasn't.

Curious, she nodded. "Sure. But only a few. I don't want you to ruin your dinner."

The instant Jarrod trotted away, Scott shoved his hands in his pockets, his expression sheepish. "I should have warned you on the phone, except I couldn't think of a diplomatic way to phrase it. So I'll tell you flat-out. Gram's main goal these days is to see me married. Don't be surprised if she drops a few broad hints along those lines or regales you with my sterling qualities." One side of his mouth hitched up. "She's an incorrigible romantic, and at this stage of her life I doubt she's going to change. So I'll apologize in advance if she comes on too strong with any matchmaking stuff. Just ignore it."

Because he wasn't interested? Or because he wanted to save her the embarrassment? She had no idea.

Nor should she care. It wasn't as if she was in the market for romance. Right?

Summoning up a smile, she ignored the annoying swirl of disappointment in the pit of her stomach that suggested otherwise. "Maybe it's an encouraging sign she's still thinking along those lines. If she'd given up on life totally, I doubt she'd care."

"That's one way to put a positive spin on it, I guess. Just brace yourself. She put her glasses on this afternoon, and because she hasn't bothered with them for weeks, I'm assuming she wants to get a good look at you."

"Forewarned is forearmed."

Jarrod bounded back clutching several silver-wrapped Kisses. "You want one, Mom?"

"No, thanks, honey."

"Mr. Walsh?"

"Don't mind if I do." He fished one out of her son's palm and peeled back the paper. As he popped it in his mouth, he grinned at Cindy. "A treat before the trick."

She chuckled and followed him toward his grandmother's room.

At the threshold, he knocked on the half-closed door. "Gram? We're here. Are you decent?"

"Come right in. I've been waiting for you."

Scott pushed the door open, ushered Cindy and Jarrod inside, then entered and edged past them to make the introductions.

As Cindy walked forward to grasp Barbara Walsh's extended hand, she did a quick assessment. In some ways, the frail woman propped up in bed was what she'd expected. Thin, with close-cropped white hair and a fragile appearance, she reminded Cindy of a newly hatched bird, all bones and skin. But her grip was firm, her voice was strong and the eyes behind her wire-rimmed glasses were keen.

She might be down, but she wasn't as out as Scott seemed to think she was.

"Nice to meet you, Mrs. Walsh." Cindy smiled as they shook hands. "And please excuse my attire. We spent the afternoon hiking and came directly from the park."

"Please, call me Barbara. And no apologies necessary. My husband and I used to love to hike. Stan always said it was edifying for the soul to spend time in nature's cathedral. Those redwoods are awe-inspiring." She craned her neck to size up Jarrod. "Hello, young man. I heard you were only eleven, but you look much more grown up than that."

Jarrod had been hovering half behind her, but as Cindy turned, his chest puffed up ever so slightly and he edged out. "I'll be twelve in two months. Would you like some candy?" He lifted his hand toward the older woman

"Now that would be a treat. Thank you." She selected one of the chocolates—softened from the warmth of his palm, Cindy suspected, as the woman scraped off the silver paper. "We eat too early here, and the only dessert was Jell-O." She wrinkled her nose, put the Kiss in her mouth and smiled as she chewed. "This is much better."

"Would you like another one?" Once more, Jarrod extended his palm to display the two remaining candies.

Scott's grandmother patted his arm. "You're a very generous boy, but you go ahead and enjoy those while your mother and I chat." She refocused on Cindy. "Why don't you have a seat near the bed, my dear, so we can get acquainted?"

Cindy started toward one of the two cushioned chairs in the room, planning to pull it toward the bed, but Scott beat her to it. As he maneuvered it into place, Barbara beamed at him.

"He's always been such a gentleman. Treats

me like a princess, too. Can you imagine what a wonderful husband he'd make?"

As Scott straightened up, he gave Cindy a "what-did-I-tell-you?" shrug. She took the seat, doing her best to suppress the grin tugging at her lips.

"That's much more cozy." Barbara folded her hands over the blanket. "First of all, thank you for the lovely flowers." She gestured to the bouquet on her nightstand. "They were such a nice surprise. And so considerate. Scott thought so, too. Didn't you?" She adjusted her glasses and peered over at him as he stood at the foot of the bed.

"Yes. Very nice."

"It was my pleasure." Cindy smiled at the older woman. "After all, I did spend the night in your house. And I was very impressed by your paintings. You have a real gift."

A flush rose on Barbara's cheeks. "I did win a ribbon or two in my day, but that was long ago. I haven't painted at all since Stan died." Her heightened color faded and she plucked at the edge of the blanket.

Cindy's throat tightened, and on impulse she leaned forward and covered Barbara's hand with her own. "I know how bleak things can seem when you lose someone you love."

The older woman nodded. "Yes, I'm sure you do. Scott told me you were a widow, too."

"That's right. There are still days I'm surprised when I walk into the kitchen in the morning and he's not sitting there with the paper, eating his bagel with strawberry cream cheese." Moisture gathered in her eyes, and Cindy blinked to clear her vision.

"I know what you mean, my dear. I've had the very same experience. True love never dies. On the other hand, the heart has an infinite capacity to love." She cast a meaningful look from Cindy to her grandson. "But I didn't ask you here today to dwell on sad things. Scott's told me about your job and the display you have to create. He thinks the trunks in my attic might be of help to you."

"Yes. From what he's said, it sounds as if I could build a whole theme around the material he found. I'd love to take a look at it."

"Then by all means I think you should. As soon as possible. Scott—" she transferred her attention to her grandson "—why don't you take Cindy and Jarrod to the house right now and let her check it out?"

"Now?" Scott did a double take.

"Why not? Your deadline is approaching, isn't it?" Barbara directed her question to Cindy.

"Yes, but..." Cindy didn't want Scott to feel

railroaded into spending what remained of his Sunday in a dusty attic. "Scott probably has other plans for the rest of the day." She addressed her next comment to him. "If you wouldn't mind leaving a key somewhere, I could run over in the morning and have a look after you go to work."

"Nonsense. That attic is a rattrap. I wouldn't want you traipsing around up there alone. And if there's any moving or heavy lifting to be done, Scott's your man. He's got plenty of muscles."

True. Even in a dress shirt there was no disguising his broad chest and well-developed biceps.

"Does that mean I could play with Toby?" Jarrod joined the conversation.

"Of course you could." Barbara jumped in before Scott or Cindy had a chance to respond.

"Cool. Can we go, Mom? Please?"

No way did Cindy intend to further impose on Scott. But as she opened her mouth to decline, he spoke.

"As long as you're this close, it wouldn't hurt to take a quick look."

"Oh, boy! Let's go now!" Jarrod was already halfway to the door.

"Yes, you all go on your way. And Cindy, if you still want to show my paintings to that gallery-owner friend of yours, go ahead and take some digital pictures of them while you're there. I'd be curious to see what she has to say."

"Sold." Scott circled around to the other side of the bed and gave Barbara a kiss on the forehead, but his gaze met Cindy's as he bent.

I warned you. Just go with the flow.

At least that was the message she thought he was sending.

"I guess we're going to your house." She rose as she addressed the older woman.

"A fine end to a Sunday. And if you find anything interesting in those old trunks or have any questions, let me know. I remember a few bits and pieces about Elijah and Emma. It will be fun to revisit their story. Scott, if these two have spent the day hiking, give them some dinner. They must be hungry."

"Oh, no, we're fine." Cindy shot Scott an apologetic glance. "We always take granola bars with us. We can eat when we get home or grab a bite along the way."

"Don't be silly." Barbara dismissed the comment with a flip of her hand. "Scott hasn't had dinner yet either. No sense him eating alone. He does enough of that as it is."

"I *am* pretty hungry, Mom." Jarrod shot her a hopeful look.

"There, you see? Scott, why don't you get a

take-and-bake pizza at Big Louie's and put it in the oven while you show Cindy the trunks and Jarrod entertains Toby?"

"We'd better leave or she'll be planning our dessert for us, too." Scott rolled his eyes at Cindy as he picked up her chair to return it to its usual spot.

"Too bad there isn't any of my carrot cake in the freezer."

"Now that would be a treat." Scott set the chair down and turned to Cindy. "She makes a killer carrot cake. I was just thinking about it yesterday." He moved to the foot of the bed and addressed his grandmother. "You know, if you'd concentrate on your physical therapy, you could come home and bake me one."

The spark in her eyes dimmed. "My carrot-cake-baking days are over." She took Cindy's hand. "It was lovely meeting you, my dear. Let me know what you find in the trunks and what your friend says about my paintings."

"I will. Thank you for sharing your family history with me."

"It was my husband's family. But as I recall from the old stories Stan's aunt used to tell, Elijah and Emma had quite a romance that began a bit later in life. That gives me hope." She cast a deliberate look at her grandson.

"Ready, Cindy?" Scott inclined his head toward the door.

"Yes."

Barbara lifted a hand in farewell to Jarrod. "Goodbye, young man. You give Toby a pat for me. And come back and see me sometime."

"Okay. Thanks for letting me play with him."

Jarrod exited, and Cindy followed him out. Scott joined them a few moments later, closing the door halfway behind him.

As Jarrod bounded ahead, Scott fell into step beside her. "Don't say I didn't warn you."

"I'm sure her intentions are good."

"What's the old saying about a road that's paved with those?"

Was he suggesting romance in general was akin to fire and brimstone? Or just a romance with her? Was there an unhappy relationship—or marriage—in his past? Was he divorced? Had he written off romance? If so, why?

None of those questions should matter to her.

But as they parted in the parking lot to go to their respective cars, Cindy had to admit they did.

Chapter Seven

To his surprise, despite the stop he made at Big Louie's, Scott beat Cindy and Jarrod to Gram's house.

He slid the pizzas onto the counter and surveyed the kitchen. He hadn't planned on visitors when he'd left for church this morning, and his half-filled coffee mug on the table, along with a crumb-littered plate and a jam-covered knife, attested to the fact he'd been running late.

If he was lucky, he'd have time to clean up and change clothes before they arrived.

Less than five minutes later, as he was pulling a T-shirt over his head, the doorbell chimed. After grabbing his socks and shoes, he padded barefoot down the hall.

Cindy gave him a once-over as he pulled the door open, her gaze lingering on his bare feet.

"I was wondering if you got lost." He stepped back and motioned them inside. "Come on in."

She cleared her throat and waved a bag at him as she and Jarrod entered. "We stopped to pick up dessert. I'm sure it's no competition for your grandmother's carrot cake, but I wanted to contribute something to the meal. Especially since you were coerced into inviting us. Sorry about that."

"Not a problem." He shut the door and led them to the kitchen. "Gram's right about eating alone. I do it too often. Jarrod, why don't you check on Toby while I show your mom the stuff in the attic? He knows I'm home because he's been scratching on the door, but he'll be much happier to see you. There's a ball somewhere in the yard he likes to play with."

"Yeah. I found it the last time." The boy took off for the door at a trot.

A few seconds after he exited, a muffled bark and a whoop of laughter floated back inside.

Scott sat on a kitchen chair and grinned at Cindy, who was keeping her distance, hands shoved in the pockets of her jacket.

"Give me a sec to put on my shoes. I went straight from church to visit Gram, and the attic isn't the place for nicer clothes. Not that you don't look nice, of course."

In truth, she looked fabulous. Her slender jeans flattered her trim figure, and the soft knit

T-shirt under her jacket highlighted her curves. He knew because she'd slipped out of the jacket at Gram's. However, she'd left it zipped up here. All the way to her neck.

Had Gram's broad hints made her more uncomfortable than she'd let on at Seaside Gardens?

"Thanks." She dipped her chin and fiddled with the zipper. "But these are just old hiking clothes. I don't care if I get them dirty."

He tied his second shoelace and stood. "I hope you don't have a dust allergy."

The hint of a smile twitched at her lips. "I'd be in trouble if I did, working at a history museum. We deal with a lot of old artifacts that haven't been cleaned in years."

"Okay. Then let's take a look."

A few minutes later, under the small circle of light provided by the single, low-watt bulb hanging in the attic, Cindy dropped to her knees on the makeshift planks of wood that served as flooring and leaned close to touch the captain's chest.

"Wow. Look at that dovetailing. Plus the original rope handles with Turk's-head capitals. It's even got an angled front, which is rare."

Excitement over the find had chased away

her nervousness, and his own tension dissipated. "You really know your stuff."

She shrugged, still focused on the chest. "There was a lot of sea trade along the coast years ago. And before rail service began in 1914 the only way to get to San Francisco from here was by boat. Since I joined the historical society I've been reading up on area history, and the sea played a large role. But as far as I know, we've never focused an exhibit on the Cutter Service."

"Ready to look inside?"

"Absolutely."

Scott turned the key and lifted the lid.

"Oh, my." Her words were hushed. Reverent. "May I touch things?"

"I did. Help yourself."

Gently she traced the outline of the carved heart inside the lid, then stroked the coat and lifted the corner to examine the items beneath it before checking out the nautical objects on the other side.

"Logbook, personal journal, letters..." She turned to him, and despite the dim light he could see the sparkle in her eyes. "This is an amazing cache. There might be enough here to build the whole exhibit around, focusing on the Cutter Service but personalizing it by telling the story through the eyes of your great-great-grandfather."

"And don't forget Emma." Scott shifted around and lifted the lid of the dome-shaped trunk.

"Wow again." She leaned past him to get a better look at the old-fashioned wedding gown.

Even the stale air in the attic couldn't mask the fresh, floral scent that wafted toward him as her arm brushed his chest, and he found himself bending closer to her soft blond hair for a better whiff.

"Emma's, I assume?"

It took a moment for her question to register—and a few more for him to form a coherent response. "That would be my guess." His reply came out husky, and he swallowed as he straightened up. *Get a grip, Walsh.* "I didn't want to poke around too much in that one. I was afraid the dress might disintegrate."

"That's possible. All of this needs very careful handling." She sat back on her heels. "Until I can go through the contents, I won't know for certain if there's enough here to carry a display, but I'd guess there is. Can we move these trunks out of the attic?"

"You and I can't. They're too heavy. But I can get my neighbor to help me. Where would you like them?"

She caught her lower lip between her teeth. "We could take them to the historical society for processing. Or I could do an initial pass here to verify it's the treasure trove I think it is. That might be better. I'd hate to go to the trouble of hauling them across town only to discover I don't have what I think I have."

"Unlike Gram, I don't use the dining room. Would that work?"

"Perfect. I can bring over some archival supplies from the office tomorrow."

"Why don't I give you the spare key? You can come and go as you please while you sort through everything."

She hesitated, playing with the zipper pull on her jacket. "I don't want to intrude on your home."

"It's Gram's home. I only moved back in to save money on rent and for security reasons. An occupied house is less appealing to burglars. And I guarantee Gram will approve of the idea. She liked you." He closed the lid of the dome-topped trunk.

She did the same with Elijah's. "I wouldn't want to mislead her about…us." Based on the sudden uncertainty in her voice, her excitement had morphed back to nervousness.

So Gram's matchmaking had, indeed, unsettled her more than she'd let on earlier.

"Don't worry. I've been up-front with her

from the beginning. She knows there's no romance involved."

Why not?

He saw the question in the glance she tossed at him, and he stared back at her as she averted her head to hide the surge of color on her cheeks.

How about that?

He'd meant to reassure her with the statement. Up until now, despite the chemistry zinging between them, he'd gotten her clear keep-your-distance message. And it had dovetailed nicely with his vow to avoid women with young children.

Now this.

Did she realize she was communicating longing…invitation…loneliness…with her eyes?

She brushed her fingers through the dust on top of the lid. "I guess we'd better put that pizza in. Those Hershey's Kisses aren't going to hold Jarrod much longer."

Though she seemed to be trying for a casual, conversational tone, the slight quaver in the last word gave her away.

He took a deep breath, fighting a sudden urge to take her in his arms. Hold her close. Stroke her hair.

Kiss her.

Not smart, Walsh.

Gritting his teeth, he kept his hands occupied by pressing his fingers to the floor to steady himself.

When he didn't respond, she twisted toward the collapsible stairway and started to rise to a crouched position in the low-ceilinged attic. But in her haste to escape she caught the toe of her sport shoe on the edge of one of the rough flooring planks and tottered.

Instinctively, Scott swiveled toward her and caught her upper arms, stabilizing her. She dropped back to her knees, facing him.

Mere inches away.

He got lost in her deep blue irises as he inhaled her appealing scent. Traced the faint sprinkle of freckles across her nose. Felt her quivering beneath his fingers.

Somewhere, deep in the left side of his brain, logic was shouting at him that a dusty attic wasn't a romantic setting. That he was making a mistake. That he needed to back off.

Yet he couldn't curb the impulse to lift his hand and touch the gossamer softness of the hair framing her face.

Cindy drew in a sharp breath—but she didn't move.

Pull back! Now! Before it's too late!

The urgent command echoed in his mind.

He heard it. Knew he had to follow it. Otherwise, he'd put two more hearts at risk.

Summoning up every ounce of his discipline, he clenched his jaw and prepared to back away.

That's when Cindy leaned into his hand.

The pressure of her cheek against his palm was subtle—and perhaps unconscious.

But it was an invitation nonetheless.

Then her eyelids drifted closed.

Scott's lungs stopped working. Willpower only went so far. He wasn't made of steel.

Giving up the fight, he leaned toward her. Close. Closer. A whisper away. His own eyes closed. One more second and…

"Hey, Mom! Where are you?"

Cindy gasped and jerked back.

"Mom?"

Color high, Cindy yanked her gaze from his and scrambled toward the opening in the floor. "Up here, h-honey. In the attic." She twisted and swung her legs over to the ladder, descending as fast as she could.

And she didn't look back.

But Scott's pulse continued to gallop.

Man.

Sitting back on his heels, he ran a shaky hand through his hair.

What on earth had just happened? How could

his resolve to keep his distance evaporate with one touch?

He didn't like the answer that presented itself. But neither could he dispute it.

After a mere two weeks, he was attracted to Cindy—big-time. And the temptation to let things escalate, to test the waters, was escalating.

But what if he gave in to it only to have the electricity between them fizzle? Cindy would be hurt, and Jarrod had already suffered one loss that had turned his world upside down, sent his grades into a tailspin and necessitated counseling. What would a second loss do to him?

He couldn't pursue Cindy. It was too risky—and selfish.

Plus, he didn't need any more guilt in his life.

Suddenly weary, Scott pulled the chain on the light and crossed to the opening in the floor. As he started down the stairs, the murmur of conversation drifted from the kitchen, Cindy's musical tones mingling with Jarrod's high-pitched voice. A welcome sound in this quiet house. One he could get used to.

But despite Gram's prodding, it was better all around to focus on friendship rather than romance with Cindy.

Even if his heart wanted more.

* * *

"Can I give him one bite, Mr. Walsh?"

Cindy played with her second piece of pizza, only half listening to the exchange between Jarrod and their host.

"Just one." Scott took a sip of his soda while Toby planted himself beside her son's chair, tail swishing the floor, nose tipped up, attention riveted on the piece of pizza in Jarrod's hand.

"Here you go, boy." Jarrod tore off a hearty bite and fed it to the dog, who chomped it down, then gave a contented purr deep in his throat. "Your treat for the day."

Treat for the day.

The words echoed in Cindy's mind as she thought about that charged moment in the attic when she'd practically asked Scott to kiss her. What had she been thinking?

That, in a nutshell, was the problem. There had been no thinking involved. Only feeling.

"More pizza, Cindy?" Scott pushed the large cutting board containing what was left of the second pizza toward her.

"No, thanks. I've had plenty."

That wasn't true—and they both knew it. She'd managed to chew and swallow the first slice, but she hadn't made much progress on the second one. After hiking in the woods for hours, she should be starving.

Instead, her stomach was queasy.

"Let's move on to those cupcakes then." Scott rose and picked up their plates. "I peeked in the bag while the pizza was baking. They look good."

"We got white and chocolate." Jarrod bounced up and pulled the molded plastic container of six cupcakes out of the bag. "We didn't know which kind you like best."

"Either one is fine with me. You pick first."

"Chocolate." Jarrod returned to the table, popped the lid and selected the one with the most icing, as Cindy knew he would.

She was glad some things were predictable.

"Coffee?" Scott picked up a mug from the counter and lifted it toward her.

"Yes, thanks." Maybe some caffeine would jump-start her brain.

He delivered their mugs one at a time, as he had the morning he'd served her breakfast, favoring his damaged hand. She tried not to stare, but she couldn't help wondering once again what had caused the extensive scarring.

"How did you hurt your hand, Mr. Walsh?"

As Jarrod voiced the very question that was on her mind, she jumped in before Scott had a chance to respond, her tone sharper than she intended. "It's not polite to ask personal questions, honey."

Her son's face reddened and he dipped his chin.

"It's okay. I don't mind answering it." Scott slid into his seat and wrapped his fingers around his mug, sending Jarrod a reassuring glance. "My hand was crushed a few years ago in an accident on a job site. It took a lot of operations and a lot of therapy to get it back in shape. Or as good a shape as it's ever going to be." He set the mug down and flexed his fingers. "Not bad, considering the doctors had to piece the bones back together like a puzzle. I don't have as much sensation in my fingers as I used to because of nerve damage, but at least it works. So how's that cupcake?"

"Good." Jarrod ran his finger through the icing and stuck the glob in his mouth. "I busted my arm once."

"Yeah? How'd you do that?" Scott broke off a bite of his cupcake as her son dug into his with gusto, his discomfort evaporating under Scott's matter-of-fact reaction to his question.

Cindy took a sip of her coffee, her admiration for the man ticking up yet another notch.

"Fell off my bike." The words came out garbled as Jarrod chewed his cupcake. "Mom and Dad had to take me to the emergency room. But it works fine now." He demonstrated by holding it out and shaking it.

Apparently thinking this was a new game, Toby began leaping into the air and barking.

"Whoa, boy." Scott restrained him with a hand on his collar. "Now that you've gotten him excited, you're going to have to take him out again and let him run off all this energy."

Cindy swallowed and gripped her mug. She didn't relish any more alone time with Scott today.

"Okay." Jarrod shoved the last quarter of his cupcake into his mouth and jogged for the door.

"Ten minutes." Cindy called out the warning, fighting down her panic. "I have things to do at home."

Acknowledging her comment with a wave of his hand, Jarrod exited, a yapping Toby at his heels.

Quiet descended in the kitchen. Only the hiss of water dripping from the coffeemaker and the muted ticking of a clock in his grandmother's living room broke the stillness.

In desperation, she searched for some innocuous topic that would buy her the time to gulp her coffee, choke down a few bites of cake and escape.

But her host had other ideas.

"I think we should talk about what almost happened."

The piece of cake she'd just swallowed got stuck in her throat, and she fumbled for her water glass. Took a long swallow.

Okay. She could handle this. They were mature adults. And maybe it would be better to acknowledge the elephant in the room rather than ignore it. "I guess that's not a bad idea. Especially if our paths are going to start intersecting."

"That's my thought." He leaned forward and clasped his mug. "I can't say precisely what ignited that spark in the attic a little while ago, but the fact is it's been there almost from the beginning. On my end, anyway."

Honesty deserved to be repaid with honesty. No matter how uncomfortable it made her feel. "On mine, too."

One side of his mouth quirked up. "I thought so, but thank you for confirming that my instincts are still sound. Here's the thing. You're a very attractive woman. You're kind, conscientious, hard-working, intelligent—in other words, from everything I've been able to gather in our short acquaintance, you're the real deal. Under other circumstances, I wouldn't have waited for Gram to matchmake. I'd have asked you out already. But A, I don't think you're ready to date yet, and B, there's a problem on my end."

She remained silent as he rose, crossed the room and topped off his mug. Instead of returning to the table, however, he propped a hip against the counter. Keeping some distance between them.

"Nine months ago a woman I'd been dating for three years gave me an ultimatum. Make a commitment or get out of her life. And she was right to do that. Three years is plenty long enough to know if you're heading for anything permanent. Too long, actually. I knew a few months after we met there were issues that could keep things from getting serious, but the relationship was comfortable, I was busy and it was easier to maintain the status quo."

He took a swig of coffee, set the mug down and gripped the edge of the counter behind him, facing her. "When I broke things off, Angela was disappointed and hurt—but not surprised. I think she'd already figured out that was how things were going to end. However, her eight-year-old daughter, Leah, was devastated. She'd bonded with me far better than she'd ever bonded with Angela's ex, who'd disappeared not long after she was born. And I'd been part of her life for almost as long as she could remember. Angela wanted a clean break, and I understood that, but I'll never forget Leah's anguished face the night I told her I wouldn't be coming around anymore."

His voice rasped and he turned around to grope for his mug—with the wrong hand. It slipped from his fingers and shattered on the floor, spewing coffee and glass all directions.

Muttering a word she couldn't make out, he yanked the towel off the oven handle and bent to sop up the mess.

Cindy rose and pulled several paper towels off the rack before joining him.

"I can clean this up." His words came out gruff as she knelt on one knee and began to wipe the shards of glass into a pile. "I don't want you to cut yourself."

"I'd like to help." With more than spilled coffee. But this was the only assistance she could offer at the moment. In silence, she continued to gather up the broken pieces.

Once the coffee was sopped up and all the remnants of the shattered mug were collected, he retrieved a dustpan from the utility closet, swept up the shards and deposited them in the trash.

Cindy went back to her seat at the table, giving him back his space for the conclusion of his story.

To her surprise, however, he closed the distance between them and stopped behind his chair, gripping the back with his fingers.

"So here's the bottom line. After that experience, I vowed never again to get involved with a woman who had young children. It was bad enough to hurt Angela, but it tore me up inside to hurt Leah. I wouldn't want to inflict that kind of pain on Jarrod if we began dating and things didn't work out. He's been through more than his share of bad stuff in the past year and a half. He doesn't need to start counting on somebody who might not be around in six months—and you don't either."

As Cindy digested all he'd said, she came to two conclusions.

Scott was right to proceed with caution—for everyone's sake. Even if she found herself wishing he wasn't.

And not many men would make—and keep—a vow to protect the hearts of others at the expense of their own happiness.

Which only made the man standing across from her even more appealing.

She swiped at a smudge of icing on the table as she collected her thoughts. "I appreciate your candor—and your principles."

"Not to mention my flattery." He gave her a smile that seemed a bit strained.

"That, too." She swallowed past the tightness in her throat. Might as well be honest. "Too bad things couldn't be different."

"Yeah."

"I hope we can at least be friends."

"I hope so, too."

But she heard a touch of uncertainty in his words. Steve had told her once that when a man had romantic feelings toward a woman, all hope of simple friendship was gone. She suspected Scott felt the same way.

The back door opened, and Jarrod stuck his head in. "Is my ten minutes up yet?"

"More than." Cindy rose, snagged her purse from the back of her chair and slung it over her shoulder. "Let's put the pedal to the metal."

Jarrod blinked at her, then broke into a grin as he gave Toby a final pat. "That's what Dad always said when it was time to go."

She frowned. Yeah, it was. How odd. She'd never used the expression before. Why now? Was her subconscious reminding her that Steve hadn't been gone that long? That it was too soon for a new romance anyway?

"Why don't you take the cupcakes home, Jarrod?" Scott snapped the lid shut, slid the container back in the plastic bag and handed it to her son. "I don't need the calories."

"Is that okay, Mom?"

"Sure." Fishing in her purse for her keys, she moved toward the door.

Scott beat her to it, opening it as they approached.

"Thanks again for dinner, Mr. Walsh. And for letting me play with Toby. Maybe we can do it again sometime."

Over Jarrod's head, Scott looked at her, as if to say, *That could be dangerous. Jarrod could get hurt.*

Hearing the unspoken message, she stepped in. "We're all busy, honey, and this is a long drive. It probably won't happen very often."

Her son's face fell. "I guess not. I had fun tonight, though." He trudged toward the car.

"Here's the house key." Scott held it out to her. Their fingers brushed as she took it, and her heart skipped a beat. "Come by whenever it's convenient. I don't usually get home until after seven."

"Okay. Thanks." The words came out breathless. Telling. "I'll bring my camera tomorrow and take a few shots of your grandmother's paintings, too, if that's all right."

"No problem."

She took a step back. "Well…I guess we'll be off."

"Drive safely." He jammed his hands into his

pockets. As if he was fighting the temptation to reach out to her.

"Good night." Turning, she strode toward the car.

Once inside, she fitted the key in the ignition. A long streak of dried icing on her finger caught her attention, and pushing worries about germs aside, she licked it off.

The taste was sweet on her tongue.

But as she put the car in gear and allowed herself one last peek at the tall man standing in the doorway watching them leave, she couldn't help thinking that Scott's kiss would have been even sweeter.

Chapter Eight

Scott stopped at the door to Gram's room and narrowed his eyes.

Something was different.

The view, that was it. Gram always kept the blinds drawn. Tonight, they were open. The sky was washed with gold from the setting sun, and the newly planted flower box outside her window was bursting with spring color.

What was up?

Venturing into the room, he looked over at the bed.

Another first.

Gram was reading one of the paperback novels that had been gathering dust for months.

Cindy's good news had apparently had the positive impact he'd hoped it would.

As he approached the bed, Gram peered at him over the top of her glasses. "You're late."

"Hello to you, too." He pulled one of the chairs closer to the bed, gestured outside and sat. "Nice view."

"Very. I've always liked the light at the end of the day. So warm and comforting." She set her book down and changed the subject. "Did you get delayed at work?"

"Yeah. It was a bear of a day. Make that a bear of a week. And it's only Wednesday. We've had one glitch after another." He stifled a yawn and circled back to the more important topic. "What's with the book? And the blinds?"

She gave a dismissive wave, but bright spots of color bloomed on her cheeks. "You spent hard-earned money on those books. Figured I ought to read a few. And you're paying for the view. Might as well enjoy it."

"Glad to hear I'm finally getting my money's worth. Did Cindy call you?" He knew she had. She'd left a message yesterday on his home answering machine saying she would.

"Yes. Charming girl. I'm delighted your great-great-grandparents' chests have helped her out with her exhibit."

"They didn't just help her out. They're the foundation for it."

"It's about time they proved useful to someone after taking up storage space in my attic all these years. She's going to bring a few things over for me to see in a day or two. You know about the paintings, I assume?"

"Yes. Cindy included that news in her voice mail. Sounds as if Janice is quite taken with your work."

Gram squinted at him, clearly disgruntled. "Voice mail? You mean you haven't talked with her?"

"No. She's a busy woman."

"Hmph." She creased the edge of the blanket with her fingers. "So what do you think of this painting business?"

"I think it's great. I predict Janice will sell every one you send." A proceed-with-caution warning flashed in his mind, reminding him to temper his enthusiasm. Subtle encouragement was okay, but pushing would be a mistake. "Too bad there's a limited supply."

"I've been thinking about that." Gram adjusted her glasses and rested her hands on the book. "I expect I might have time to do another piece or two before the Lord calls me home. And I still have all my supplies. They're in the basement."

"Yes. I saw them. I could bring some over if you'd like. The light's not too bad in here."

"No, it's not." She surveyed the view from her window. "I suppose I might do a little dabbling. It would help pass the days. Why don't you gather up a few brushes and my paints and a couple of canvases? There are plenty of blank ones down there."

Thank You, God!

"Sure. I'll root around tonight."

"Don't go to any trouble on my account."

"It's no trouble, Gram."

"Well, don't put yourself out." She leaned back. "Have you heard from Devon lately?"

"No. I've left two messages since I sent the money, but she hasn't called me back. Have you talked with her?"

"This morning. She didn't get that part she was after, and she lost her waitress job because she kept canceling at the last minute to go to auditions. I bet you can guess where this is heading."

"She needs a few bucks to tide her over until she gets another waitress gig."

"Give the boy a gold star. She knows better than to ask me, though. I'm tapped out. I told her not to ask you either, but I expect that fell on deaf ears." Gram sighed and shook her head. "Hindsight is twenty-twenty, as they say. We were too soft on her after the accident. Never made her stand on her own two feet. I love that girl with all my heart, but she needs to grow up and accept responsibility for her own welfare. As for you—" she pointed a finger at him "—you need to stop enabling her."

"Enabling?" Scott's lips twitched. "Where did you pick up that lingo? Have you been watching *Dr. Phil?*"

She scowled at him. "I may be old, but I keep up with things. And I'm right about this."

"I didn't say you weren't."

"But it's hard to say no. I know." She blew out an exasperated breath. "Well, you work on that. And while you're at it, work on your love life, too."

Vintage Gram. Feisty and outspoken and interested in life. The very thing he'd been praying for.

But he'd have to keep his diversionary skills in tip-top shape from now on.

Standing, he stretched, then retrieved her walker. "In the meantime, let's take a stroll."

Much to his surprise, instead of arguing she put the book aside, threw back the blanket and slid her legs over the side of the bed. Without his help.

"I believe I'd like to get a few of those Hersey's Kisses at the nurses' station. Let's go there first."

"No argument from me."

As she took off with more energy and speed than usual, Scott sent another silent thank-you to the Lord. The prognosis was definitely looking up for the woman who'd played such an important role in his past.

Too bad the same couldn't be said about the role of a lovely single mom in his future.

"What a night!" Cindy pushed through the door to the Mercantile and tossed the remark to Lindsey, who was seated on a stool behind the counter. "Between the Friday-night traffic and the fog, the drive up from Eureka was the pits."

"I'll bet. No one's going very far in this tonight, that's for sure." The other woman swiveled around to peruse the swirling fog outside the window. "Not that I want to discourage business, but I hope you don't have much shopping to do. You need to get home as fast as you can and hunker down."

"I'm with you. Just eggs and orange juice for tomorrow morning. Jarrod always looks forward to a big breakfast on Saturday, and I hate to disappoint him. I'll be out of here in three minutes."

With a flip of her hand, she hurried toward the refrigerated case at the back of the store—and almost ran into Scott as she turned the corner of the aisle.

"Whoa!" He grabbed her arm with one hand

to steady her and juggled a deli sandwich and soft-drink can in the other.

"Sorry." She caught her balance, backed up a step—and tried to convince herself the sudden uptick in her pulse was because of the close call rather than the man standing in front of her.

"No harm done." Scott dropped his hand from her arm and moved aside for her to pass in the narrow aisle.

Steeling herself, she squeezed past, trying to ignore his muscled chest, the five-o'clock shadow darkening his jaw, and the distinctive scent of his aftershave.

No luck. Her pulse continued to misbehave.

"By the way, thanks for the message you left about Gram's paintings and the stuff in the trunks. Sounds like things are working out all around. Gram's spirits have taken a definite upswing."

Cindy kept moving until she was a safe distance away. "I know. I stopped by after work tonight. She'd asked for a photocopy of Elijah's journal, and when I dropped it off she was sitting by the window, sorting through her paints. There was a new sparkle in her eyes."

"Thanks to you."

Cindy lifted one shoulder, trying not to take his praise too personally. "Let's give God the credit for inspiring me to show her paintings to

Janice." The old-fashioned clock in the Mercantile bonged, marking half past seven, and as the time registered she wrinkled her brow. "Aren't you here awfully late?"

"Tough week."

That explained the fine lines of weariness radiating from the corners of his eyes.

"But you can't drive back in the fog. Visibility is close to zero."

"I know. I got the last room at the Orchid. But I missed the sisters' grilled salmon." He hefted the items in his hand and grinned. "A poor substitute, but I'll live."

The man who'd plied her and Jarrod with food and hospitality on more than one occasion was planning to eat a cold sandwich for dinner after putting in a grueling week.

That wasn't right.

Yet the alternative scared her.

As if reading her mind, he backed toward the checkout. "I don't want to delay you. Even driving a few blocks in this stuff is dangerous. Be careful." He started to turn away.

"Wait." The word came out before she could stop it.

He pivoted back toward her.

Too late to back out now. "Look, Jarrod and I are eating late tonight, too. We're only having spaghetti, but you're welcome to join us. At least it would be a hot meal."

Scott hesitated, and Cindy half hoped he'd refused.

But he didn't.

"Spaghetti sounds a lot better than this." He lifted the sandwich again. "Thanks."

"Okay. Let me grab a couple of things."

He joined her at the refrigerated case, and while she selected her eggs and orange juice he put his sandwich and soda back. Then he followed her to the checkout counter.

"Long three minutes." Lindsey grinned as she rang up Cindy's purchases and eyed Scott.

"My fault. I delayed her." Scott propped a hip against the counter and folded his arms.

"I thought you were buying some stuff for dinner." Lindsey checked out his empty hands as she made change for Cindy.

"No."

"He's, uh, eating with us." Cindy took the change and tucked it in her purse.

"Mighty neighborly." Lindsey grinned at her. "You all have a nice evening."

"Thanks." Scott picked up the bag and they exited into the fog together, the bell over the door jingling as they left.

"I only live four blocks from here." Cindy

tightened her jacket around her as the cool veil of mist enveloped them.

"I'll follow you."

At her car, he handed over the groceries after she slid in. "Don't lose me, okay?"

With a one-sided grin, he closed her door and disappeared in the fog toward his own car.

And sixty seconds later, as she drove slowly toward home, his headlights no more than murky shadows behind her, she found herself wishing his parting comment applied to more than a drive through the fog.

"That was much better than a cold deli sandwich. Thank you." Scott folded his napkin, placed it next to his empty plate and smiled across the table at Cindy.

"Mom makes great spaghetti." Jarrod sucked up the last few strands—reminding Scott of himself at that age—and turned his attention to his mother. "Are we having chocolate chip cookies for dessert? I saw the dough in the refrigerator this morning. I bet you made it last night after I went to bed." He sent her a hopeful look.

"Do you have any room left?" She rose, picked up her plate and reached for his.

"I always have room for cookies."

"I'll second that." Scott stood, too, and picked up his plate.

"You don't have to help." Cindy held out a hand for his plate, but he moved it out of her reach.

"I'm used to cleaning up after myself. Besides, what's the old saying about many hands?"

"Make light work." Jarrod wrinkled his nose as he finished the adage.

"That's the one."

"Dad used to say that a lot." He got to his feet and gathered up the Parmesan cheese and empty bread basket—then stopped. "Hey... who's going to feed Toby tonight?"

"My neighbor. I already called. He does that for me once in a while if I have to go out of town."

"Do you do that a lot?" Jarrod followed him around the center island toward the sink area.

"No. The company that's building Inn at The Point is in San Francisco and I have to go down there for a meeting every few weeks. But I'd rather be home."

"Me, too." Jarrod opened the fridge and tucked the can of cheese on a shelf. "My dad traveled a lot, but he liked it."

"He had to travel because of his job, honey." Cindy began loading the dishwasher. "His favorite time of all was hiking in the redwoods with you, though."

"Yeah. I miss that."

Scott handed the plates to Cindy, intrigued. Had she mentioned the redwoods to bolster Jarrod's memories? Or had that, indeed, been her husband's favorite time? And if so, what did that say about their marriage?

"We've been going again a lot in the past few months."

"I know."

But it's not the same.

Jarrod didn't have to say the words for the unspoken caveat to resonate in the room.

A shadow darkened Cindy's irises, changing them to the color of the sea before a storm. He started to reach out to her. Caught himself. Dropped his hand and returned to the table.

Time to change the subject.

"So what's your favorite movie, Jarrod?" He gathered up the salt, pepper and butter.

"I like *Robin Hood* a lot. The old one from the '30s."

"With Errol Flynn?"

"Yeah. Have you ever seen it?"

"Years ago."

"You want to watch it again? Or a different one? My dad had a whole collection of old movies."

"I'm sure Mr. Walsh doesn't want to stay that

long, Jarrod. The fog's bad and he needs to get back to the Orchid."

Was she booting him out? It was hard to tell, with her face hidden behind the sweep of her hair as she leaned over the dishwasher.

But he wasn't ready to leave yet. Even if that was the wise thing to do.

"A movie might be pushing it, but I wouldn't mind hanging around for those cookies. If that's okay."

Cindy straightened up and pushed her hair back, her expression apologetic. "Of course. I just didn't want you to feel obligated to hang around."

"Can I put on the movie while they bake, Mom?"

"We just watched that one."

"I never get tired of it."

"A boy after my own heart." Scott smiled at him.

"You want to see our collection?"

"Good idea. Show him the movies, Jarrod." Cindy spared him a quick glance as she rinsed her hands in the sink. "It's an impressive collection. I'll get the cookies going."

Her ploy to put some distance between them was obvious. As was the reason for it. While they'd had an honest, rational conversation about their mutual attraction, that hadn't diminished the electricity. The sparks had been flying throughout the entire meal.

Maybe they did need a time-out.

He followed Jarrod through the great room and down the hall of the contemporary two-level home. It was grander than he'd expected, and the furnishings were high quality, from the granite countertops in the kitchen to the Brazilian walnut floors on most of the first level. A dramatic hanging stairway led to a second-floor balcony that overlooked the great room, which boasted a soaring, vaulted ceiling.

Cindy's husband must have done okay with his consulting work.

So why had she gotten a job outside the home after he died when it was obvious she wanted to spend more time with Jarrod?

While her son showed him the extensive vintage film library and popped the DVD in, he mulled over that puzzle. And continued mulling it over until Cindy summoned them for dessert.

Jarrod beat him back to the kitchen, and the boy was already piling cookies on his plate when he entered.

"Can I take these into the family room, Mom? The movie's running."

"Don't you want to stay and visit with our guest?"

At the youngster's guilty look, Scott smiled at

Cindy. "It's hard to compete with Errol Flynn. I don't mind if he wants to watch the movie. I'm not staying long anyway."

"All right." She grabbed a napkin from a holder on the center island. "But try to keep the crumbs contained."

He ran off, milk, cookies and napkin in hand.

"Help yourself." Cindy gestured to a rack of cooling cookies. "I can make coffee if you'd like."

"What are you drinking?" He strolled over and put three of the warm cookies on one of the dessert plates she'd set out.

"I'm a milk-and-cookies girl myself."

"Count me in." He grinned and set his plate on the granite-topped island, then straddled a stool. "It will take me back to my childhood. One of my favorite after-school treats was milk and homemade cookies. Gram was quite a baker."

"Maybe she will be again."

"That's what I'm praying for."

"For the record, I've added my voice, too. Where two or three are gathered and all that." She finished pouring the milk, handed him a glass and perched on the stool beside him.

"I appreciate that." He bit into the crumbly cookie, closing his eyes as the soft chocolate dissolved on his tongue. "Man, this is great.

Don't tell Lindsey, but they're even better than hers. And I should know. I buy a few every time I go to the Mercantile."

"That's only because these are warm."

"I don't think so." He examined the cookie. "These have pecans, don't they?"

"Yes."

"That's what gives them the edge." He took another bite, wondering how best he could satisfy his curiosity about the state of her finances. Subtlety was key. "Nice house, by the way."

Cindy perused the upscale kitchen. "Actually, I'm thinking about selling it once the market improves and life settles down."

"How come?"

She broke one of her cookies in half and gathered the crumbs together with a fingertip. "It's expensive to maintain, and I prefer smaller, cozier places. This was Steve's dream house, and with him gone it feels…empty."

His dream house. Not hers.

Another interesting insight.

But he was still curious about the money issue.

"So is that why you went back to work? The house expenses?"

To his relief, she didn't seem to resent the query. "Partly. Steve's insurance paid off the house, but we didn't have a lot of savings. Any extra money went into a college fund for Jarrod, and I'm not about to touch that. We figured Steve had a lot of working years left and there'd be plenty of time to worry about securing our own future. Funny how life can surprise you."

No kidding.

"I can't even imagine what a shock it must have been when you lost him."

"Shock doesn't begin to capture it. And poor Jarrod...I don't think he slept a full night through for months. Steve was gone a lot for work, but he and Jarrod were great buddies. He was a wonderful father and a good husband."

Wonderful father. *Good* husband.

Scott finished off his third cookie. "Does Jarrod ever..." His cell phone began to vibrate, and he pulled it off his belt. "Sorry. With all of Gram's problems, I always check caller ID."

"I understand."

He scanned the number. Devon. Just as Gram had predicted.

With a sigh, he let it roll to voice mail and put the phone back on his belt.

"Problem?"

"You might say that. Also known as my sister. I'll call her back later."

"Your grandmother mentioned she was an actress in New York."

Since she'd opened the door, he decided to step inside. "Did she tell you anything else?"

"No. I did get the impression she wasn't too pleased with her, though."

"That's putting it mildly." Scott swiveled sideways on the stool to face Cindy, resting one foot on the horizontal support bar. "It's kind of a messy story."

She gave a soft laugh devoid of humor. "Life itself can be pretty messy. And every family has warts. I didn't mean to pry…"

"You didn't." He cut her off in a firm voice. "To be honest, I wouldn't mind having someone besides Gram to bounce the situation off of, if you're willing to listen."

"I'd be happy to. Talking things through can often bring clarity."

True. So who did *she* talk things through with?

After brushing his hands off over his plate, he rested his forearm on the counter. "My parents were killed in a car accident when I was eight. I was out here visiting Gram and Gramp at the time. Devon was only three, and she was in the car, too. It was touch-and-go with her at first, and we all treated her with kid gloves while she recovered—and from then on. But I think our pampering has come back to bite us."

He gave her a quick recap of the latest dramatics in his sister's life. "So I'm assuming she's going to hit me up for cash again. And to be honest, with all of Gram's expenses, there isn't any to spare."

"You're paying the bills at Seaside Gardens?"

His neck warmed. "Only since Gram's nest egg ran out."

Cindy's eyes softened. "Another valid reason for her to sing your praises."

The heat crept higher. "Anyone would do the same for someone they loved."

Her skeptical expression told him she didn't believe that. But she let it pass.

"You know, we had a similar situation in our family. My brother had a difficult time settling down, too. He had a full scholarship to college, but he threw it away halfway through his sophomore year to become a ski bum in Colorado. He was three years older than me, and I remember how he was always hitting Dad up for money. Dad sent it for several years, motivated in part by guilt, I think. We lost my mom when we were young, and Dad always thought he hadn't spent enough time with us. I suppose supporting my brother alleviated some of his guilt. Which was misplaced anyway. He was a great father.

"Anyway, he finally realized he wasn't doing Jack any favors. He applied some tough love and stopped sending the money. I could see how hard it was on him to say no, but he stuck to his guns. Left to his own devices, my brother ended up straightening himself out. He enrolled in a trade school, became a carpenter in Kansas City, went back to church and met a wonderful woman. They have two children now. He'll never be rich in the eyes of the world, but he has everything that matters. Everything Dad hoped he'd have. And Dad lived long enough to see him get his act together and for them to reconcile."

Scott gathered up a stray cookie crumb and deposited it on his plate with the others. "That's what Gram thinks I should do. It's nice to know that choice could have a happy ending. Thank you for…"

"Hey, Mom, can I have two more cookies?" Jarrod zoomed around the corner and skidded to a stop.

"How many have you had already?"

He scrunched up his face. "I can't remember. Maybe four?"

"One more."

"Oh, Mom!"

"One." She took a sip of milk, raising her eyebrows at him over the rim of the glass.

He huffed out a breath. "I feel like Toby. One treat at a time."

Scott smothered a chuckle behind his napkin, then cleared his throat and stood. "On that note, I think I'll say good-night."

"Will you tell Toby hi for me?" After a thorough inspection of the remaining cookies, Jarrod selected the largest one.

"I'll do that."

"Thanks. See ya." He raced back toward the family room.

"Let me walk you out." Cindy rose and started to turn toward the front of the house.

"Wait." Scott touched her arm, and when she twisted back toward him he dabbed at her upper lip with a napkin. "Milk mustache."

Her eyes widened, and he felt himself falling into their sapphire-blue depths.

She moistened her lips.

His mouth went dry.

Talk about a dumb move. He needed to get out of here.

Fast.

Tossing the napkin back on the counter, he fished in his pocket for his keys. "It should be an interesting trip back to the Orchid." He'd hoped the words would sound relaxed. Instead, they came out ragged.

"Just drive slowly." She waited while he circled the island to pluck his jacket off a bench against the wall, then took the lead to the front door as he shrugged into it. "Would you call after you get there? Otherwise, I'll worry."

"Sure. Thank you for dinner and the cookies."

"Small repayment for all your hospitality to us."

A tendril of fog swirled into the room, and Cindy shivered. His cue to leave.

"I'll call in a few minutes. Thanks again."

Tugging up the collar of his jacket, he dived into the fog. In seconds, the lights of the house behind him were reduced to a faint, ethereal glow. They disappeared completely by the time he reached his car and slid behind the wheel.

But thoughts of the appealing woman inside didn't vanish so easily.

He sighed.

It was going to be a long, lonely night.

Chapter Nine

"Sorry, Devon. The well's dry." Scott adjusted the pillow behind his head and stared at the ceiling in his room at the Orchid. It might only be ten-thirty in Starfish Bay, but it was one-thirty in the morning in New York. Yet his sister sounded wide-awake—just as he'd been since dropping into bed at nine-thirty.

Thanks to a certain single mom who'd given him a serious case of insomnia.

"But I lost my job. I told you, I..."

"Devon." He'd already listened to her sob story. He didn't want an encore. Nevertheless, he tried to maintain a friendly, reasonable tone. "You'll have to get another one."

"Good-tipping waitress jobs aren't that easy to come by in New York."

"There are other jobs."

"Like what?"

"You have a teaching certificate and a degree in theatre. Why not teach acting?"

"I don't want to teach. I want to perform."

"There's no reason you couldn't do that on the side."

"You mean community theater stuff?" Her voice was stiff with disdain.

"It would give you a creative outlet and still allow you to make a living."

"Teaching jobs are hard to get, too."

"That may be true in New York, but there are other cities and towns."

"I'm an actress, Scott."

"You also have to eat."

Silence.

He wiped his hand down his face and waited her out as the wind moaned through the spruce trees behind his room.

"How come you're being so hard-nosed all of a sudden?"

"I'm not being hard-nosed. I'm being realistic. I don't have any spare cash. Gram's money ran out six months ago and I've been footing the bill for Seaside Gardens ever since. That's why I moved back home—to save on rent money. I've already dipped deep into my emergency funds. I can't support you, too. You're smart and talented and capable of doing something great with your life—but professional theater doesn't appear to be it. You've given it ten years, Dev. You've had some nice parts, but you aren't making a living at it. Maybe it's time to move on."

Scott's fingers clenched around the phone and he closed his eyes, waiting for the hang-up click that would communicate her miffed reaction.

But she surprised him.

"I didn't know money was that tight. You never said anything before." Her voice was subdued and touched with…shame?

Perhaps there was hope for her yet.

"I didn't want to bother you with my problems. And I'm sorry the acting thing hasn't worked out. You have the talent to be a star, but there are a lot of talented people who never get their name in lights. That's life. Dreams are wonderful, but at some point you have to let them go if they don't work out."

"I still think I could make it. If I had the right break." A hint of stubbornness resurfaced in her inflection.

They were back to square one.

"I'm not saying you couldn't. I'm just saying you'll need to find another source of funding from now on."

Several more beats of silence ticked by.

"You're not going to give in this time, are you?"

"No."

A long, dramatic sigh came over the line. "Okay. I need to think through everything you dumped on me."

"I'm here if you want to talk."

"Yeah. I know. You've always been there whenever I've needed you. I'll be in touch."

She severed the connection, and Scott pressed the off button. She'd sounded so forlorn at the end. Should he send her a few bucks to tide her over while she sorted through...

No!

He didn't want to be an enabler.

He needed to apply some tough love.

The two women in his life agreed on that. And they were right.

Setting the phone on the nightstand beside the silk orchid in a bud vase, he flipped off the light, flopped onto his back—and frowned.

The two women in his life?

When had Cindy begun to occupy such a key role?

The answer eluded him...but the implication didn't.

Like it or not, she'd become part of his world. As had Jarrod.

But as long as he didn't act on that fact, everyone would be safe.

Even if that also meant he'd be lonely.

What a gorgeous day.

As Cindy parked and slid out of her car in front of the Orchid, she inhaled a lungful of the spruce-scented air. The cloudless blue sky and sparkling sea off The Point gave no hint of the fog that had draped itself over the headland and coastal town last night. This afternoon, visibility was close to a hundred percent.

Jarrod stepped out from the passenger side, his disappointed gaze on the empty parking lot in front of the adjacent motel. "I guess Mr. Walsh left."

She hoped so. That's why she'd waited until late in the afternoon to run this errand. She didn't want to risk another encounter that would leave her tossing into the wee hours two nights in a row.

"He only stayed overnight because of the fog, honey. I'm sure he headed out bright and early." She closed her door and started for the door. "Let's get those cinnamon rolls, okay?"

"Yeah. The Orchid has the bestest ones in the world. I'm glad you called, or they'd all be gone."

"Genevieve promised to save me two. It

wouldn't seem like Easter tomorrow without Orchid cinnamon rolls after church, would it?"

"Nope."

The dinner crowd was already beginning to gather, and Genevieve waved a menu at them from across the foyer as they entered. "Your rolls are behind the counter. I'll get them for you in a jiffy. Just let me seat these nice people." She smiled at the young couple beside her and ushered them into the dining room.

Cindy strolled over to the counter, but Jarrod beat her there. As her son helped himself to a few M&M's from the always-brimming bowl beside an arrangement of silk orchids, the front door opened behind them.

"So how was your dinner?"

At Lindsey's question, she turned.

"What dinner?" Genevieve was back already. She skirted the counter and retrieved a white bag from underneath.

"Scott missed your salmon last night, and Cindy took pity on him after she ran into him buying a deli sandwich at the Mercantile." Lindsey plucked a candy from the bowl and popped it in her mouth.

"Is that right?" Genevieve rang up Cindy's purchase on the old-fashioned cash register. "I didn't think to ask him about dinner last night when he checked in. It was crazy. Can't recall the last time we had a full house in April. We would have rounded up some food for him—though I'm sure he enjoyed dinner at your place more, Cindy."

Her cheeks warmed, but before she could respond, Jarrod spoke up.

"Yeah, we had a lot of fun. We ate spaghetti and Mom made chocolate chip cookies. It was even better than the pizza and cupcakes we had at his house last week."

At Jarrod's announcement, Genevieve and Lindsey exchanged a look.

Great. Now everyone in Starfish Bay would know about her impromptu dinner with Scott in Eureka, too.

"It was business, actually." Cindy handed the money to Genevieve, striving for a casual tone. "Scott found some old trunks in the attic that belonged to his great-great-grandfather, and he thought they might give me some ideas for an exhibit I have to do at work."

"Yeah. He was a sea captain. Mr. Walsh gave Mom a key to his house so she could go through the stuff in the trunks."

Her son was a font of information today.

She picked up the bag and edged toward the door as she corrected Jarrod. "It's his grand-mother's house, honey. And he's at work when

I'm there. I'm about to transport everything to the historical society anyway."

"Such a nice man." Genevieve beamed at her.

"Handsome, too." Lindsey grinned.

She was out of here.

"I need to run." She groped for the handle of the door.

"Not too fast, I hope." Genevieve shook a finger at her. "A little bit of hard-to-get goes a long way."

Cheeks flaming, she escaped through the door to the sound of the women's chuckles, Jarrod close on her heels.

"What does *hard-to-get* mean, Mom?"

Leave it to her son to pick up on that phrase.

"It's an old saying." She slid into the driver's seat, stalling as hc hopped in on the other side. "It's kind of a game. Like…teasing. Pretending you don't want something when you really do, to confuse someone."

Jarrod's brow wrinkled. "Why would you do that? If you want something from someone, shouldn't you just tell them?"

In a simple world, yes.

But her world wasn't simple.

A new relationship would come with guilt and baggage and risks to Jarrod, as Scott had pointed out.

None of which she needed.

But she wasn't about to go into any of that with her son.

She shoved the key in the ignition and started the engine. "You're right, honey. It's kind of a strange game."

Nor was she playing it, no matter what Genevieve and Lindsey might think. She and Scott knew where they stood with each other. They'd been honest about their feelings.

Yet there had been a sin of omission on her part. There were certain truths she hadn't shared—nor been willing to admit...until now.

As she put the car in gear and pulled onto Highway 101, she faced the first one: the attraction she and Scott had acknowledged was becoming bigger. Deeper. At least on her end. And it was bringing with it a boatload of guilt. How could she be so disloyal to her husband this soon after his death?

That led her to the second truth. One she'd been dancing around for weeks. Somewhere along the way, as Steve's consulting business had grown and he'd travelled more and more, they'd drifted apart. There'd been no cataclysmic breakdown, no harsh words ever exchanged. She'd continued to love and respect him, and he'd been a fabulous father, but their relationship had grown stale. She couldn't remember the last time she'd felt excited in his presence. Even in the beginning, the spark between them had never been as potent as the one between her and Scott.

Which increased her guilt exponentially.

If only…

"Mom! You missed our street!"

At Jarrod's exclamation, she jammed on the brake, swung into the parking lot of Jaz's biker bar on the other side of town, and made a U-turn.

"Whoa! That was cool!" Jarrod looked over at her, gripping the dashboard. "I guess you were daydreaming, huh, Mom?"

"I guess I was. And that's not a smart thing to do while you're driving."

Or anytime else when it came to a certain attractive construction guy.

Where was Gram?

The bottom fell out of Scott's stomach as he surveyed her empty room. Had she fallen again? Was she back in the E.R.? Why hadn't anyone called him? He'd seen her yesterday for the facility's Easter services and brunch, and she'd been fine.

He swung around, strode into the hall and hailed a passing aide he didn't recognize. No surprise there. The staff turnover at this place was astronomical. It was a huge challenge to keep up with all the newcomers.

Planting his fists on his hips, he blocked her path as she glanced up from the clipboard in her hand. "I'm looking for my grandmother, Barbara Walsh. She's not in her room."

The young woman's eyes widened at his clipped delivery, and she took a step back. "I—I'll check with the desk."

"Never mind. I can do that."

She scurried away, clearly intimidated by his stance and irritation. A twinge of guilt tugged at his conscience, and he hesitated. He hadn't meant to frighten her—but neither was he going to take the time to apologize. Not until he found out where Gram was.

He continued toward the nurses' station, only to be intercepted at a T in the hallway by an aide he *did* recognize—accompanying Gram as she pushed her walker toward him.

"Well, look who's here!" Vivian smiled at him as they drew closer. "And don't we have some good news today."

"I don't know why everyone's making such a fuss just because I decided to start physical therapy again." Gram avoided his eyes and kept moving.

"You went back to physical therapy?" Scott stared at her. On top of that news, she'd ditched her nightclothes for a pair of capris and a sweater that had been gathering dust in her closet for months.

"Move aside or I'll run you over." Gram shooed him away with a flap of her hand. "And I'm in no mood for a discussion. I hurt."

"You're supposed to hurt. It's not working if you're not hurting." Vivian patted her shoulder. "But a couple of pain relievers will take care of those aches. Pretty soon, you'll be strolling along without this thing." She tapped the walker.

"That's my goal." Gram looked over her shoulder after she passed Scott. "Why are you here so early anyway?"

"The rain shut us down for the day." He fell in behind the duo.

Vivian motioned him forward. "Why don't you take over spotting duty while I run and get those painkillers?"

He took the aide's place and studied Gram, not liking the pinch of pain around her mouth. "Did you check with the doctor about this?"

"Of course I checked with the doctor. He was all for it. An hour later, they'd assigned me to Brett, and let me tell you, he's a looker. If I'd known they'd put me with someone like him, I'd have gone back to therapy a lot sooner."

Scott's lips twitched. "How old is this guy?"

"Old enough to be my great-grandson. But I can enjoy the view, can't I? Makes me feel young again. And does that boy know how to flirt! You could take a lesson or two from him."

As they entered her room, he stopped again. He'd been so distraught by her absence he hadn't noticed the easel and canvas by the window or the paints on a small table beside it. An impressionistic seascape was already beginning to emerge.

"You've been busy."

She crossed to the bed, slowly lowered herself to the mattress and expelled a long breath. "Ah. Better." She waved at the walker. "Take that thing and put it over in the corner. I hate the sight of it. Always have. Brett and Vivian think I may not need it if I buckle down with the therapy."

Exactly what he and the doctor had been telling her for months—to no avail.

But the aide and physical therapist weren't responsible for Gram's change of heart. Cindy got full credit for that—along with his undying thanks.

"Maybe I better not put the house on the market after all."

"Let's not get carried away. But I suppose we might want to delay that step a bit. Why don't you pull up a… Ah, Cindy! You made it!"

Scott swung around and found Cindy hovering on the threshold. He'd attribute her presence to another matchmaking attempt, except Gram hadn't known he was going to show up early.

No matter, she'd surely find a way to take full advantage of the opportunity.

"I don't want to intrude while Scott's here." Cindy remained at the door, her expression uncertain.

"Nonsense. You come right in. Isn't this a cozy coincidence?" Gram gave them a delighted smile.

Scott could think of other words for it.

Skirting around to the other side of Gram's bed, Cindy addressed him. "How come you're not in Starfish Bay?"

"Rain delay."

She cast a glance out the window at the overcast sky, and twin grooves appeared on her brow. "I better not linger if it's raining up north. The fog might roll in again."

"I could always offer you a spaghetti dinner." Scott smiled, captivated by the intense blue of her irises—the same color as the sea off The Point on a sunny day. "Though it wouldn't be as tasty as yours."

"You've had Cindy's spaghetti?" Gram's eyes lit up.

Uh-oh.

He hadn't told her about his impromptu dinner at Cindy's the night he'd been stuck in Starfish Bay.

"I took pity on him when I saw him buying a deli sandwich in the general store the night the fog stranded him." Cindy shot him a sympathetic look, set the overstuffed satchel in her hand on a chair and changed the subject. "I brought you copies of a few of Emma's letters, but be warned—her old-fashioned handwriting is as difficult to decipher as Elijah's. Transcribing his logbook has been slow going. I'm going to focus on that, plus his journal and Emma's letters, this week—starting tonight. I made copies of everything for myself, too." She pulled a folder out of the satchel and passed it to Gram.

Defenses up, Scott prepared to run interference if Gram returned to the subject of their spaghetti dinner.

Much to his surprise, she didn't.

"I've been reading his journal for the past few days. You're right. It's a slow process, and my eyes aren't what they used to be, but I have to say Elijah had a way with words. I especially liked the April 4, 1898 entry—the one he wrote while he was at sea protecting vessels during the Klondike gold rush. You should take a look at that one. Is the original journal still at the house?"

"Yes. I'd like to finish processing everything there. I hope to begin transporting items to the historical society next week."

"Excellent." She turned to Scott. "You check out that entry, too. You might learn a thing or two."

Scott raised an eyebrow. "About the gold rush?"

"No." Gram pinned him with an intent look. "But it *was* about treasure."

Although he had no idea what that meant, he suspected it had something to do with Cindy.

"Well…" Cindy hoisted her shoulder purse higher. "I need to beat the fog, but I did want to share one other piece of exciting news. Janice told me there was a young couple in the gallery last weekend, and both the husband and wife were very taken with your painting of Humboldt Bay. She thinks they might be back to make an offer on it."

For a moment Gram was speechless. "Now wouldn't that be a kick after all these years?"

"Janice also wanted me to invite you up anytime to visit the gallery. She'd love to meet you."

"Oh, I haven't been anywhere much except the doctor's and the E.R. since I fell." Gram gave a dismissive wave. "That's too long a drive."

"Genevieve and Lillian would like to meet you, too. And the food at the Orchid is fabulous.

You should taste their cinnamon rolls. As for the blackberry cobbler…" Scott looked toward the heavens. "Wow."

"I must say, you two are tempting me." As she regarded them, Scott could almost hear the gears grinding in her brain. "I believe I might consider it. Maybe next weekend. If Cindy will introduce me to Janice and give me a tour of the town?"

Cindy's rueful gaze connected with his, verifying she was as attuned to Gram's matchmaking efforts as he was. "There's not much to see. Starfish Bay is a tiny village stretched along 101 with a family-friendly biker bar at one end, the Orchid at the other and a few shops in between. A tour would take all of ten minutes."

"It sounds charming. And afterward, you and Jarrod could join us for lunch at the Orchid. Then Scott could return the favor by showing us around his job site. I'd like to see this inn I've been hearing about."

"I'm sure Cindy has better things to do with her weekend than spend hours with us, Gram."

"She said herself the tour of the town won't take but a few minutes, and she and Jarrod have to eat anyway. Why not at the Orchid with us?"

Checkmate.

To his relief, Cindy seemed more amused than annoyed.

"Your logic is hard to refute, Barbara."

Gram tapped a finger against her head. "My body might be old and stiff, but my brain is as agile as it ever was."

"And then some," Scott muttered.

"I heard that." Gram sent him a withering look, then turned her attention back to Cindy. "It would be such a nice treat, my dear. My first real excursion for pleasure since I moved into this place. Scott's been after me to get out for ages, but I haven't been tempted until now."

Cindy bit her lower lip, and he could guess what she was thinking. She knew how important it was to him to get Gram interested in life again, but she also knew they were being manipulated.

Yet the excursion would do Gram a world of good. And what could happen with Genevieve, Lillian, Janice and Jarrod around?

Apparently Cindy came to the same conclusion because she smiled and shrugged. "I'd be happy to show you around. Would Saturday work for you?"

"Any day is fine. My social calendar is flexible. You work out the details with Scott." Gram reached over and took Cindy's hand. "I'll look forward to the visit, my dear. Thank you. And drive safely going home. Scott will walk you out."

"Oh, he doesn't need to bother." She took a step toward the door, clutching the satchel with both hands. "I don't want to disrupt your visit any more than I already have. I'm fine on my own."

"Of course you are. You're a capable, intelligent woman. But a gentleman always walks a lady to the car—and Scott is a gentleman."

Circling the bed, he lowered his voice as he bent to relieve Cindy of her satchel. "Don't fight the current."

"I heard that, young man. My ears still work, too."

As Cindy smiled, he chuckled and addressed his grandmother. "Don't go on any more marathon walks while I'm gone."

"Don't worry. I'm done for the night. And you take your time. I'll amuse myself with these letters Cindy was kind enough to bring." She tapped the folder in her lap.

Guiding Cindy out of the room, Scott held his tongue, waiting until they were out of earshot before he spoke again. "Sorry about that."

"Don't be. I can spare an hour or two Saturday if it will help motivate your grandmother."

"Thanks to you, she's already motivated. She went to physical therapy today for the first time in months, and she dressed in street clothes."

Cindy detoured around a wheelchair parked

in the hall, its occupant slumped over asleep. Furrows creased her brow. "She doesn't belong here, Scott."

"I know—and I think she's beginning to admit that, too."

As they crossed the lobby, a rumble of thunder shook the building.

Cindy shivered. "Looks like we're in for more unsettled weather."

He pushed the outside door open, following after she exited. The weather wasn't the only thing that was unsettled, he thought, as he walked beside her to her car, her faint floral aroma mingling with the scent of rain, her blond hair swinging close to his shoulder.

She used the remote to unlock her car as the first raindrops began to fall.

"Perfect timing." She slid behind the wheel and he handed her the satchel. "You better get inside or you'll be drenched."

"I'll call you about Saturday."

"Okay."

She reached for the handle, forcing him back. With a wave, she pulled the door closed, backed out and drove toward the street.

He remained standing there until her tail-lights disappeared in the direction of Starfish Bay. And he didn't hurry back inside, despite the rain. He needed a few minutes to breathe the fresh, tangy air and regroup.

Because every time he saw Cindy it was harder to let her walk away.

But he couldn't let Gram pick up on that. He didn't want her to get carried away with this whole romance thing.

Even if *carried away* was an accurate description of how he was beginning to feel.

Chapter Ten

Cindy's vision misted, and she rose to fish a tissue from her purse on the counter. Dabbing at her eyes, she slid back into her seat at the kitchen table and scanned Elijah Adams's journal entry from April 4, 1898 for the second time.

I read your letter from yesterday again this evening, my dearest Emma. You will never know how your tender sentiments sustain me during our long separations. On this voyage, they are also helping me bear the terrible grief we share. I wish I could speak with you this moment, but I must be content to put my thoughts in writing for you to read when I return, just as you have poured your gentle, loving spirit into these precious letters, which I cherish and eagerly anticipate opening each week whenever the miles and the sea come between us.

Parting has always been difficult to bear, as you know, but never more so than our last goodbye, mere days after we bid our darling Chloe farewell and commended her to God. I know you continue to suffer, as I do, and to question why the Lord would snatch away our firstborn—our only child—the delight of our days—after four short years. I can find no reason for what seems to be such a cruel betrayal to faithful servants.

Yet I trust in His grace and goodness implicitly, as I know you do. So I do as I have always done in times of trial. I ask Him to bless us both with courage and fortitude, and to give us strength to endure. That prayer offers me great solace, but how I wish I could also hold you close and comfort you whilst seeking my own comfort in your loving arms.

We always knew our life together would bring both joys and sorrows. That fate might not always be kind. That our love could be tested. And surely we have known all of these things. For like the shifting sandbars and the narrow, treacherous passage that leads to the sea from our own Humboldt Bay, life holds many hidden perils.

But despite my desolation this night, I know I would have chosen no other path. Just as the seafaring life was my destiny, so, too, are you. Your love is the sextant that gives my life direction. The light on shore that guides me home. The stars above that help me stay the course. You are my everything, dearest Emma, in good times and in bad. For from you I have learned the truth of what St. Paul wrote two centuries ago: Love never fails. And it is worth even the risk of loss.

Cindy's throat tightened, and she blinked as a wave of fresh tears blurred her vision. If the ribbon-bound letters Emma had sent along with Elijah to be opened each week during his absences were half as powerful as her husband's journal entries, she'd be a basket case before she finished reading them. For their story was the stuff of romance novels—a sustaining, enduring love strong enough to reach across a century and resonate with vibrant passion and steadfast devotion.

As she closed the folder containing the copy of Elijah's journal, Cindy understood why Scott's grandmother had called out that particular passage this afternoon. Though Barbara might not be privy to all the reasons she and Scott were avoiding romance, it was clear she hoped this long-ago couple would convince them true love could overcome all obstacles.

And as Cindy rose and turned out the lights for the night, she had to admit Barbara's strategy was beginning to make inroads on her heart.

The question was, did Scott feel the same way?

Balancing a mug of coffee in his good hand, Scott yawned and padded barefoot toward the dining room. Might as well track down that passage in Elijah's journal Gram had bugged him about earlier. She'd be all over him tomorrow night if he reneged on his promise to read it.

Another yawn snuck up on him. Five minutes, max. That was all he'd give it. Then he was crashing.

Toby trotted along beside him, flinching at every boom of thunder, and Scott bent to give him a pat. "Hang in there, boy. It's only noise. But you can stay in the kitchen tonight."

The pup already knew that. The minute he'd entered, he'd spotted the blanket-padded box Gram kept in reserve for bad nights. Scott had gotten a vigorous tail-wag in thanks for hauling it in from the garage.

Letting the dog sleep inside instead of in his cozy house in the backyard had been another promise Gram had finagled out of him, but he'd been happy to make that one. The fact she was worried about Toby being out in the storm was a positive sign.

He stopped beside the dining room table and surveyed the room Cindy had taken over. The two trunks stood against one wall, and neatly labeled boxes were stacked against another. The table held some of the more fragile items, including the journal, logbook and letters, along with the faded ribbon that had bound Emma's missives to her husband. A decrepit antique photo album was off to the side, and though he was curious about the contents, he was afraid to so much as breathe on it.

After taking a sip of coffee, Scott set his mug on the credenza beside Gram's treasured Waterford apprentice bowl. He ran a finger over the dusty rim, a smile whispering at his lips as he recalled his grandparents' surprise when he'd presented them with two first-class tickets to Ireland, tucked into a pot of candy gold bullion, on their fiftieth anniversary. Not a week since had passed without Gram polishing the souvenir of that treasured trip. Until her fall.

But if the Lord answered his prayers, she

might be resuming that labor of love one of these days.

Turning his attention back to the table, he carefully opened the leather cover on Elijah's journal. The fragile pages appeared to be on the verge of crumbling, and he hesitated. Maybe he should call Cindy. Ask her if it was okay to handle the thing.

However, talking with her wasn't going to help him keep his distance. And she hadn't warned him not to touch it after Gram suggested he read the entry.

Decision made, he gently turned the pages, searching for the April 4 entry. He saw what Cindy had meant about the old-fashioned script being difficult to decipher. The sections of faded ink weren't going to help either.

It took him less than sixty seconds to find the passage, and as he sat down to try and muddle through it another boom of thunder rumbled through the house. Quivering, Toby whined and huddled against his leg.

"Chill out, boy. It's okay." He leaned down and gave the dog another pat as he began to read.

It took him ten minutes to get through the five paragraphs. The ornate script and odd spelling of some words slowed his reading pace. But while he had trouble translating the passage, he had no trouble understanding Gram's reasons for highlighting it.

She thought he could learn a lesson from the deep, steadfast love shared by Elijah and Emma. A love that had overcome many hurdles, including one of the biggest parents could ever face—the loss of a child.

He read Elijah's final lines again.

You are my everything, dearest Emma, in good times and in bad. For from you I have learned the truth of what St. Paul wrote two centuries ago: Love never fails. And it is worth even the risk of loss.

Throat tightening, he closed the century-old journal and rested a hand on top.

He didn't doubt St. Paul's words. True love held immense power—and it endured.

Finding it, however, was the challenge.

And he had a feeling Angela and Leah didn't think it had been worth the risk.

Suddenly weary, he stood, picked up his cooling coffee and took a slow sip. He'd thought once, in the early days with Angela, that she'd been the right woman. But he'd been wrong.

So how did you know when it *was* the right woman?

Cindy could be the one. He'd felt different

about her almost from the beginning. Yes, there'd been chemistry, but in the weeks he'd known her, that chemistry had grown into something deeper. Something that could lead to love.

Yet what if it didn't? His track record wasn't too hot when it came to discerning the real thing. Or getting out before inflicting damage if it wasn't.

A bolt of lightning lit the sky outside the window, strobing across the room. Two seconds later a loud crack of thunder shook the house. The storm was moving closer.

Inside and out.

Beside him, Toby hunkered down and buried his head in his paws, blocking out the tempest, hoping for a sunny tomorrow.

Scott could relate.

"Look, Mom! He brought Toby!"

As Cindy pulled up in front of Janice's art gallery, she glanced at the dog in the car parked in front of her, his front paws on the back of the seat, head cocked, ears twitching. He almost appeared to be smiling.

Jarrod had the door open before she shut off the engine.

"Watch the traffic!" She checked in the rear-view mirror. The scenic coastal route wasn't usually busy this time of year, even on Saturdays, but not everyone followed the law and reduced their speed as they whizzed through the town.

A slam of the passenger-side door was her son's only response.

Opening her own door with one hand, she grabbed her purse with the other as Scott slid from behind the wheel in the car in front of her.

She tried not to stare as he walked toward her, but how could she not, when he looked so handsome in his khaki slacks, cotton oxford shirt and polished loafers? She was glad now she'd bought the new capris and boat-neck knit top she'd donned this morning. Not that she'd needed them. She had plenty of clothes in her closet. Yet after she'd spotted the outfit in a store window on Thursday, she'd behaved completely out of character and made an impulse purchase.

Her reward was Scott's thorough but discreet once-over—not to mention his appreciative smile.

"You look very nice today." His smile warmed a few more degrees as she exited the car.

She resisted the urge to fan her face.

"Thanks." She brushed the creases out of

her capris, trying without success to steady her fluttering pulse. "I see you brought an extra guest." She gestured toward Toby, who was leaping about the back of the car, scratching at the window, anxious to get to Jarrod.

"A last-minute addition. I wasn't certain how Gram would react, but I think it was a smart move. At first she seemed miffed, but she ended up letting Toby ride in her lap for most of the trip." He took her elbow and guided her off the highway. "Let me help her out and we'll be set."

Cindy waited as Scott opened the back door first and clipped a leash on Toby's collar. The dog bounded out and barreled straight for Jarrod, who welcomed him with open arms.

"You're in charge." Scott handed him the leash. "You two can entertain each other while we tour the gallery. Unless you want to come learn about art."

Jarrod scrunched up his face in disgust. "I'd rather stay out here."

"That's what I figured." Scott winked at her over her son's head and turned back to the car to help his grandmother out.

Once Barbara was on her feet and steady behind her walker, he shut the door. Toby tugged at his leash, straining to join his owner, and Jarrod walked the dog over to the older woman.

Gripping her grandson's arm, she bent down and gave the pooch a pet.

"I told Scott it was silly to bring you along, but I can see you've found a new friend." The pup nuzzled her hand and gave it a slurp. "My goodness. A doggie kiss. I've missed those." Her voice hitched, and she tried to cover it with a cough.

After giving the dog one more pat, she straightened up. "Well, I'm forgetting my manners. Hello, Cindy." She extended her hand, and Cindy reached for it. "And hello to you, too, young man. I brought you a treat." She smiled at Jarrod and dug in the pocket of her slacks, pulling out half a dozen Hersey's Kisses.

"Wow! Thank you." Jarrod's eyes brightened as he took them.

"One now. The rest after lunch, honey." Cindy ignored her son's pained expression and touched Barbara's arm, indicating the window of the gallery. "Did you notice the featured painting?"

Scott's grandmother blinked at the seascape, and a smile curved her lips. "Now wasn't that nice of her? I'm anxious to meet this Janice."

"Then let's go inside." Scott took her arm as she maneuvered her walker through the door.

"Stay close, okay?" Cindy paused beside Jarrod, who remained hunkered down beside Toby, scratching behind his ears.

"Sure. Don't hurry."

By the time Cindy joined Scott and Barbara inside, Janice was emerging from the back of the shop. Once the introductions were made, the shop owner led Barbara on a tour of the gallery while Scott and Cindy followed a few steps behind.

"Thanks for bringing Toby. You made Jarrod's day. Not to mention someone else's." Cindy inclined her head toward his grandmother.

"I'm glad it worked out. I was afraid she might refuse to come after she found him in the car, but I was counting on her matchmaking agenda trumping her aggravation."

To her surprise, his last statement held more warmth than irony. Odd. In the past, when they'd discussed his grandmother's romantic maneuverings, she thought he'd been as opposed to them as she was.

Had there been a shift in his perspective?

Was he cracking the door to the possibility of a relationship?

A quick glance his direction didn't give her a clue. He was watching Gram as she chatted with Janice, the hint of a smile playing at his lips. Perhaps he was just distracted, and she was reading far more into a simple statement than he'd intended.

But what if she wasn't? What if he'd read Elijah's journal, too, and been affected by it as much as she had? What if he'd decided he cared enough about her to take another chance on love despite the risk?

If he had, that left her with one key question.

Was she ready to leave the past behind—the good, the bad and the guilt—in the hope of finding the same kind of vibrant, nurturing love Elijah and Emma had shared more than one hundred years ago?

Scott pulled into a parking spot in front of the Orchid Café, set the brake and checked out the passengers in the backseat. Cindy had hesitated when he'd suggested they leave her car in front of the gallery and use his car for the town tour and the lunch stop, but in the end logic had won out. How could she be their tour guide if they didn't all share a car? Now, Toby was squeezed in beside Jarrod, his head stuck through the window, his tongue hanging out. Cindy was regaling Gram with the history of the Orchid.

"Genevieve and Lillian came to town about

a dozen years ago and fell in love with the place. They stayed here, though it had a different name at the time. Once they found out the proprietor was ready to retire and interested in selling, they bought it on the spot. I didn't live in Starfish Bay then, but from what I've heard, they only went home to Georgia long enough to pack up. They were both widows seeking a new purpose in life, and from everything I've seen they found it in the Orchid. You'll love them."

"They cook real good, too," Jarrod chimed in.

"I'll second that." Scott pushed open his door. "Everybody crack their windows so Toby can breathe. Gram, sit tight till I come around."

He exited the car as Cindy and Jarrod slid out via her door, leaving Toby behind.

Jarrod leaned back in and stroked the forlorn dog. "I'll bring you a treat, boy. If that's okay with you, Mr. Walsh?" He shot the hopeful question to Scott as the man opened Barbara's door.

"Just one." Scott held out an arm to the older woman.

Cindy circled the car to join Scott as Jarrod gave Toby one final pet. The boy backed out of the car, giggling as the dog licked his face.

"I haven't heard that sound in a long time."

Cindy's lips softened into a smile as she regarded her son.

"Laughter is wonderful for the soul." Gram patted her arm. "For adults and children. We could all use more laughter in our lives." She sent a deliberate gaze Scott's way.

"I seem to recall an old saying about a pot and a kettle." He took her arm and guided her inside, ignoring the jab she delivered to his side.

Genevieve spotted them the instant they stepped through the door and leaned sideways to call through the pass-through. "Lillian! They're here!" Then she bustled over and hugged Gram without waiting for an introduction. "You must be Barbara. I'm Genevieve. Scott's told us all about you, and we've been so anxious to get acquainted. And isn't it lovely that Cindy and Jarrod came along, too?" She beamed at the new arrivals.

Lillian appeared from the kitchen, wiping her hands on her apron and smoothing back her hair, a streak of flour on her cheek. She smiled and took Gram's hand. "Welcome, Barbara. I'm Lillian."

As Genevieve tapped her own cheek, Lillian swiped a hand across hers. "Sorry about that. I'm baking cakes today, and the flour's flying fast and furious back there."

Energy fairly crackled off the two senior dynamos, infusing the air around them with a joie de vivre that was difficult to resist. Scott eyed Gram. Was it his imagination, or was she standing straighter than usual?

"I've been looking forward to meeting you both. What kind of cakes are you baking?"

"Double fudge, split lemon and spice. Tomorrow I'm on to pies and cobblers—apple, blackberry and pecan. Are you a baker?"

Scott jumped in. "Gram used to make a killer carrot cake."

"Is that right?" Genevieve tilted her head, her interest clearly piqued. "I love carrot cake, but we've never found a recipe half as delicious as the one our own mother used to make, and she took it with her to the grave, I'm sorry to say. We stopped trying to replicate it long ago. I'd surely like to sample yours someday."

"Oh, I haven't baked in a year. At Seaside Gardens, where I live, there's no opportunity to use a kitchen."

"My. I can't imagine not ever being in a kitchen again." Lillian said the hushed words as if someone had died, and Genevieve gave a solemn nod.

"Once you're further along in your physical therapy, maybe you can go home for an afternoon and tackle a carrot cake," Cindy suggested. "Call it selfish, but I'd love to try a piece myself."

"I suppose I could consider that down the road. But in the meantime, I came to sample *your* cooking. I've heard nothing but raves from these three." Gram gestured toward her entourage.

With a pleased smile, Genevieve picked up four menus and ushered them into the dining room. "When Scott told us he was bringing you, we put our pot roast on the menu in your honor. You don't have to order it, but I can promise it'll melt in your mouth." Genevieve passed out the menus as they took their seats at a round table by the window. "You look that over and I'll be back in a jiffy. Have you already had your tour of our charming little town?"

"Yes. Cindy was a very gracious and knowledgeable guide."

"And after lunch, I'm going to give them a tour of The Point." Scott handed back his unopened menu. "I already know I want the pot roast."

"Make that two." Gram passed her menu back, too. "I've been hearing so much about this inn Scott's building, I'm anxious to see it myself."

"Pot roast, Jarrod?" At his nod, Cindy tapped

the two menus together on the table and returned them to Genevieve. "It's unanimous."

"I must be an excellent saleswoman." Genevieve tucked the menus under her arm. "Charming spot, The Point. Lillian and I used to go down to the chapel on occasion and sit and watch the water. You'll love the view. It's quite romantic." She looked at Scott, then Cindy, whose cheeks pinkened.

Much to Scott's relief, Lillian chose that moment to hurry over with a basket of fresh-baked rolls.

For the rest of the meal, Scott guided the conversation in safe directions. With Jarrod throwing in an occasional comment and the sisters adding their two cents every time they stopped by the table, lunch passed without any more awkward interludes.

"Well, now, I'd say you did that meal justice." Genevieve bustled over to their table, Lillian at her heels, as Scott finished the last bite of his blackberry cobbler.

"My compliments to the chefs." Gram patted her mouth with a napkin and smiled at the sisters. "All of the wonderful things I heard about your cooking were true. And I like your slogan." She shot Scott a deliberate look and tapped the orchid-festooned paper placement in front of her, which displayed the words, "Wish upon a star in Starfish Bay—where dreams come true."

He ignored her.

"We like it, too. And it was certainly true for us. I hope you'll come back for another visit soon." Lillian discreetly slid the bill on the table, and Scott picked it up.

Cindy reached for her purse, but he stopped her with a touch on the arm. "My treat."

"A gentleman always pays, my dear." Gram patted Cindy's hand.

"That's very true. In my day, dutch treat was unheard of on a date," Genevieve seconded.

"This isn't a date." Cindy's tone was firm as she continued to dig for her wallet.

"I've got it." Scott handed his credit card to Lillian, and the older woman made a fast exit toward the cash register.

Cindy stopped rooting through her purse. "I'll pay you back later."

"We'll talk about it." He laid his napkin beside his plate and stood. "Right now The Point awaits."

They all rose, and Cindy let the matter drop as he helped Gram up. But he knew she wasn't pleased with his high-handedness. Nor was she happy about leaving the impression with the older women that this was a date. Because it wasn't.

But truth be told, he wished it was.

And if he could find the courage to let go of fear and guilt and take a leap of faith, perhaps next time it would be.

Chapter Eleven

"Oh, my. What a view!" Gram stared at the panoramic vista as Scott's tires crunched on the gravel road that led out of the spruce-scented forest and onto the tip of the headland.

Cindy leaned forward for a better look. She hadn't been here since construction began in January. The No Trespassing sign Jarrod had ignored was clearly posted at the chained-off entrance from 101. But the sweeping view was as spectacular as she remembered. The barren headland jutted high above the sparkling sea, and a fine mist rose from the waves crashing against the jagged rocks at the base.

"The chapel looks finished." She repositioned herself for a better view of the small white structure with the soaring steeple. Last time she'd seen it the town landmark had been in a sad state of disrepair. It appeared Louis

Mattson has lived up to his promise to dismantle, salvage and reconstruct Starfish Bay Chapel on a smaller scale.

"It better be. It was one of Mattson's top priorities. There's a wedding here next Saturday morning."

"I know. Lindsey and Nate's. This place is very special to them."

"We're invited, too." Jarrod unclasped his seat belt and bounced forward, one arm around Toby. "It'll be my first wedding. Mom says there'll be cake."

"At the reception *after* the wedding," Cindy reminded him.

"Yeah. I remember. Are you coming, Mr. Walsh?"

"No. I don't know Lindsey and Nate very well, and the chapel only seats fifty. Besides, I have to go to San Francisco next week. I won't be back in time." He pulled into a parking spot that afforded them a clear view of the emerging inn.

Cindy followed along as he pointed out the structural steel for the building. "Mattson designed this to conform with the landscape and maintain a low profile. He wanted it to blend in rather than stand out. You can see how it follows the contour of the land. It's also situated to be as invisible as possible from 101 and Starfish Bay."

"I bet this will be a pricey place to stay," Barbara commented.

"Very. Out of my league, that's for sure." Scott jingled the ring that held the key he'd used to unlock the padlock on the chain across the entrance. "Would you like to take a look inside the chapel? I have a key for that, too."

Barbara eyed the uneven terrain uncertainly. "I would, but I don't think I'm up for tramping around a construction site."

"There's a handicapped ramp on the far side." Scott put the car in gear again and drove across the gravel lot. The finished ramp came into sight as they approached, along with a weathered stone bench that Cindy suspected would serve as a great whale-watching spot. Scott pulled up close to the ramp and set the brake. "What do you think now?"

"I might be able to manage it—with a lot of help. And I would like to see inside. It's such a lovely chapel, but I'm just starting to work on ramps with Brett."

"Her physical therapist," Scott explained over his shoulder.

"Yes, I've heard all about Brett." Cindy smiled. Barbara was quite taken with the energetic young man and wasn't shy about extolling his virtues. "I can't compete with him, but I'll be happy to help in any way I can."

"Okay. We can do this." Scott opened his door. "Jarrod, clip on Toby's leash and we'll let him stretch his legs, too."

"Cool."

As Jarrod attached the leash, Scott slid out of the car and opened Cindy's door. Barbara already had her door open by the time they circled around to her. There was only room for one person beside the car, so Cindy stayed out of Scott's way. But she was close enough to admire the bunching muscles under the sleeves of his dress shirt as he pulled Barbara to her feet. Talk about being in excellent condition. The man must lift weights or work out or...

"Cindy?"

She snapped back to attention at Scott's query. "What?"

"Could you shut the door?"

From his tone, she had a feeling he'd asked her more than once.

Averting her head to conceal the sudden rush of warmth to her cheeks, she complied.

"How come your face is red, Mom?"

So much for hiding her embarrassment.

"Must be the wind. It's gusty up here." Barbara's inflection was matter-of-fact, but the twinkle in her eyes when Cindy turned back suggested she'd deduced the real reason.

Fortunately, maneuvering up the ramp required all of the older woman's attention. The going was slow, and she was puffing as they arrived at the top.

"You okay, Gram?" Scott fitted the key in the lock.

"Out of shape…is all." She grimaced. "And to think I used to play fetch…with Toby in the backyard."

"Give it time. You've progressed a lot even in the past week." Scott pocketed the ring of keys and spoke to Jarrod. "Why don't you tie Toby's leash to the railing while we peek inside? Then we can walk him around the site a bit. Ladies…" He stepped aside and ushered them in.

Barbara shuffled in first, and Cindy stayed close behind, poised to reach out if she stumbled. But they all made it inside without incident. Once they gathered in the center of the short aisle, they stood in silence as they took in the re-created space.

Extraordinary and *inspiring* were the words that popped into Cindy's mind.

Starfish Bay Chapel had been lovely when she'd first attended services here. Reverend Tobias had lavished the structure and grounds with love, and watching it decay after his death had been heartrending. But now...

She gazed at the original wooden pews, fewer in number but polished to a satiny glow. The large window in front, intersected with gold art glass in the shape of a cross, offered a sweeping view of the sea and sky beyond. She recognized the original pulpit, the brass chandeliers, the decorative molding at the top of the arched windows that lined the side walls.

It was the Starfish Bay Chapel she remembered but in miniature.

She stroked a hand over the back of a pew, the finish smooth beneath her fingers, the smell of fresh paint lingering in the air. "This is wonderful."

"I agree." Gram gripped the walker and urged it forward. "You can feel God's presence in this place. I wouldn't mind sitting a spell, if you all can spare the time."

"Fine with me. I can give Jarrod a tour of some of the equipment on the site while you soak up the ambience."

Her son's eyes widened, and Cindy telegraphed Scott a silent thank-you. Not only would that gesture make amends for their rocky start, it was every little boy's dream—getting up close and personal with heavy equipment.

Best of all, she didn't have to worry about his safety. Scott would watch out for him.

Scott smiled and winked at her. Message received.

"Seriously?" Jarrod continued to stare at Scott.

"Yes. As long as you promise to stick close."

"I promise. Can I take Toby?"

"No problem, but keep a tight grip on the leash. He's used to being fenced in, and he has a tendency to take off in wide-open spaces."

"I'll hold it real tight."

"Cindy? Would you like to come?"

"Don't be silly." Barbara waved the notion aside. "Does she looked dressed to be traipsing around in a dirt pile? She'll ruin those pretty shoes. I'm sure she'd much rather stay and keep me company."

"I think I'm staying." Cindy smiled at Scott.

"Okay. We won't be long. Let me help you get situated, Gram."

Once the older woman was settled, Cindy sat beside her in the pew.

Scott dropped a hand on Jarrod's shoulder and started for the exit. "We'll be back in a few minutes."

"Don't hurry on our account." Barbara waited until the door closed behind the duo and smiled at Cindy. "Boys and their toys. Scott's always 'iked working around heavy equipment, and if

Jarrod's a typical boy, my guess is he's going to eat this up."

"He is a typical boy, and there's no guessing involved. He'll love it." Cindy shifted sideways and rested her arm along the back of the pew. "At least it will be more pleasant than their first encounters here."

"Encounters, plural?"

Apparently her assumption that Scott had told his grandmother all about both trespassing incidents had been wrong.

"It wasn't a big deal." Cindy stalled, trying to figure out how to downplay the unpleasantness without telling a fib. "Jarrod came out here twice. Scott gave him a talking-to the second time and warned him to stay away."

"Hmm." Barbara gave her a keen look. "I have a feeling *warned* is too mild a term. He probably blew up."

The corner of Cindy's mouth quirked and she lifted one shoulder. "He does have red hair."

"True. But it's more than that." Barbara examined the front window, where the afternoon sun had gilded the imbedded art-glass cross, giving it a shimmering incandescence. "Did he tell you about his hand?"

"He just said he injured it on a job site."

Only the muted crash of the surf on the rocks

below and a distant yip from Toby intruded on the silence that followed.

Finally, Barbara sighed. "Well, I'm not one to tell tales out of school, but I can't see the harm in sharing a bit more of the story with you."

Cindy knew she ought to demure. If Scott wanted her to know his history, he'd tell her. But she *was* curious. So tamping down the guilty niggle in her conscience, she remained silent.

"Four years ago, Scott's company had a problem with vandalism on a construction site. The signs pointed to some sort of gang initiation. They beefed up security at night, but the kids kept getting in—and getting bolder. They started showing up during working hours, too.

"One day Scott spotted a young teenager fiddling with some equipment near a storage shed. He took off after him, and the boy ran into the middle of the construction site. He tripped and fell into a ditch in front of an excavator. The operator didn't see what had happened, and the kid was crushed. So was Scott's hand when he reached in to try and yank him out."

Cindy closed her eyes. After a traumatic experience like that, it was no wonder he'd gone ballistic when he'd found Jarrod at The Point. "Did the boy survive?"

"No. Scott was consumed with guilt for

months after the incident. He kept berating himself for not being quicker, for not just yelling instead of giving chase. And he was angry with the boy's parents, too. They were both successful businesspeople, absorbed in their careers, who ignored their children. That really struck a chord with him."

"Why?" The question was out before Cindy could stop it.

Barbara gripped the edge of the seat as a spasm of pain tightened her features. "I'm sorry to say my son and his wife were the same way. They never had time for Scott or Devon, which is why we brought them out here as often as we could. Scott was left on his own during his early years, and kids look for acceptance where they can find it. Unfortunately, some turn to gangs. Scott might have ended up getting in with the wrong crowd, just as the boy he chased did. He's never had much sympathy for parents who neglect their childrearing duties, and his tolerance level dropped to zero after that tragic episode."

Another mystery solved. She'd noticed the quick glance he'd flicked at her briefcase that first night in the Orchid, when he'd confronted her about Jarrod. Had watched his lips flatten in disapproval. He must have assumed she, too, was a mother who neglected her children.

Considering the rough start they'd had, it was amazing their relationship had progressed as far as it had.

As the silence lengthened, Barbara leaned closer and touched her hand, her expression concerned. "Was that more than you wanted to know, my dear?"

"No. To be honest, it explains a few things."

"I hoped it might. Scott's never been one to foist his problems on anyone else, but when you care about someone—" she arched an eyebrow and paused for dramatic emphasis "—it's important to share the good *and* the bad with them."

Barbara had slipped back into matchmaking mode.

But she was also getting tired. Cindy had been so absorbed in the woman's tale she hadn't noticed the weary droop of her mouth or her fading color.

It was time to bring this outing to an end.

"You know, I think I'll round up those two." Cindy rose and stepped into the aisle. "They could get carried away with all that equipment and leave us sitting here for hours, and I'm ready to call it a day."

"Excellent idea, my dear. I'll have a chat with the Lord while you're gone." The woman settled back in her seat and let her eyelids drift closed.

Cindy walked down the short aisle and exited into the sunlight. She scanned the construction site, spotting Scott and Jarrod in the distance, intent on examining some mammoth piece of equipment she couldn't identify.

Rather than call out to them, she crossed the expanse, sidestepping ruts and beams and ruing the film of dust collecting on her new leather flats. She'd have a polishing job tonight.

As she drew close, she tuned into the conversation.

"…was really worried about me after Dad died. Sometimes she'd hold me so tight I thought I was going to suffocate, but it made me feel better, too, you know?"

"Yeah. Hugging is one of the best ways to let someone know you care about them. And your mom loves you a whole lot."

"I know. I used to be afraid she might die, too." Her son lowered his head and kicked at a clump of dirt. "When I had nightmares, she'd come in and lay with me until I went back to sleep. It was kind of crowded, but she said she didn't mind because she was lonesome in her bed anyway. I don't think that was true, though. Dad was gone so much, she was probably used to sleeping by herself. But maybe she needed a hug as much as I did, you know? And the nightmares finally went away."

Now she didn't feel as bad about letting Barbara fill her in on Scott's background. He might not be pumping her son, but he was listening to every word Jarrod said. Just as she'd listened to Barbara.

Eavesdropping, however, was a no-no.

She drew back a few feet, out of range of their quiet conversation, and called out, "Hey! Are you guys about done?"

They turned in unison, and Toby did a happy prance, perhaps hoping the arrival of a new person would signal action rather than boring discussion.

"I think your grandmother is getting tired." She drew closer, stopping a few feet away from Scott. "We might want to head back."

"We were wrapping up anyway." Scott sent her a speculative look, as if he was wondering whether she'd heard any of his conversation with Jarrod. She did her best to maintain an impassive expression.

Jarrod tugged on her hand. "Mom! He let me climb into the driver's seat on that!" He gestured to a nearby steam shovel.

"With close supervision," Scott added.

"I'm certain of that." Cindy rested her hand on Jarrod's shoulder. "Did you say thank you?"

"Yeah. Twice. And he showed me his office, over there." He pointed at a construction trailer.

Scott grinned. "My home away from home." He gestured toward the chapel. "Shall we?"

They started across the work zone, dodging construction paraphernalia and ruts, Jarrod and Toby charging ahead.

"Be careful!" Cindy cupped her hands around her mouth.

"He's fine. There's nothing dangerous between here and there. But Gram was right. This place wasn't designed for those shoes. Watch your step." Scott fell in beside her and took her arm.

It was a polite gesture. Nothing more. She knew that.

Yet his touch made her think of his comment about hugs.

And yearn for one of his.

She faltered, and for one brief moment she was tempted to turn toward him and step into his arms.

As if sensing her thoughts, he tightened his grip on her arm. She looked over at him, and the conflict in her heart was reflected in his eyes.

Her breath lodged in her throat.

His Adam's apple bobbed.

They slowed to a stop. The world around her ceased to exist, except for the tang of salt on her lips and the muffled crash of the surf and the warmth of the sun on her face.

"Hey! Are you guys coming?"

At Jarrod's question, reality crashed back over her.

Scott dropped his hand. Stepped back. Cleared his throat. "We're right behind you."

Taking his cue, Cindy moved forward again. Telling herself to breathe.

But just when her lungs were about to kick back in, Scott took her hand and twined his fingers with hers.

This wasn't a polite gesture, meant to protect her from stumbling.

This was a deliberate message. A testing of the waters.

And she had a choice to make.

She could pull back. Play it safe. Follow the prudent path.

Or she could follow the example of Elijah and Emma and embrace the possibility of love—despite the risk.

The steeple of the chapel soared toward the sky ahead of them, and she lifted her gaze to the heavens, asking for guidance.

No message appeared in the clouds. No voice whispered in her ear. But as she followed the course of a gull drifting on the air currents, held aloft by an unseen but powerful force, she decided to follow her heart and place her trust in another powerful, unseen force.

With a gentle squeeze of her fingers, she signaled her acceptance of his touch.

And when she looked over at Scott, the warmth in his eyes seeped into the deepest corners of her soul, chasing the numbing chill away.

He didn't release her hand until they reached the chapel. And ten minutes later, when he delivered her and Jarrod back to the gallery, he took it again as he walked them back to their car.

"So who's going to watch Toby while you're in San Francisco this week?"

Once again, Jarrod's question interrupted them…but this time Scott didn't release her fingers.

"I'll ask my neighbor."

"We could watch him. Couldn't we, Mom?" Jarrod tossed the question over the hood as he circled around toward the passenger-side door. "I'm off school Friday, and I could play with him all day. We could keep each other company while you're at work."

Scott glanced at her. "I don't want to put you out."

"You know, it might work out fine. Having Toby around would keep Jarrod occupied—and hopefully out of trouble. When are you leaving?"

"Early Friday. I could drop him off on my

way to work Thursday morning before Jarrod leaves for school. He'd be okay in the basement for the day."

"Let's plan on it then."

"Great. I get back around noon on Saturday. What time's the wedding?"

"Eleven. There's a luncheon afterward. We should be home by three."

"I'll drive up later in the afternoon to pick Toby up. Why don't I treat you to dinner, too?"

He was asking her out on a date. A *real* date.

Was she ready for that?

When she hesitated, he spoke again. "Jarrod's included, of course."

Better. Having her son along would allow her to dip her toe into this dating thing—and let her back out more easily if she got cold feet.

"Okay."

"I'll call you this week."

He waited while she climbed into the car, then closed the door behind her. Once she was settled, he leaned down to speak across her to Jarrod.

"See you later in the week, buddy."

"Thanks again for letting me climb on that stuff today."

"No problem." He transferred his attention to her, his eyes mere inches away, his breath warm on her cheek. "I'll look forward to Saturday."

He stood before she could answer, but as she watched him walk away, her response echoed silently in her heart.

Me, too.

"I think Mr. Walsh likes you."

Cindy choked on the bite of turkey sandwich she'd just swallowed. Groping for her glass of water, she took a long swallow.

"It's okay with me if you guys get married."

The water went down the wrong way and she began coughing.

"Mom? Are you okay?" Jarrod half rose, his face registering alarm.

She waved him back into his seat and grabbed her napkin as she continued to cough.

He sank back, watching her worriedly until she stopped hacking.

Once she could breathe again, she took a tentative sip of water. One crisis averted.

Now on to the next one.

Resting her elbows on the arms of her chair, she clasped her hands at her waist and tried for a calm, conversational tone. "Where did that come from?"

He shrugged. "I saw him holding your hand this afternoon." He lifted the top piece of bread on the second half of his sandwich and lathered on more mustard. "Nate held Lindsey's hand in the redwoods the day they took me hiking, and they're getting married."

"Honey, just because people hold hands doesn't mean there's going to be a wedding. Mr. Walsh and I only met a month ago. We didn't even like each other very much at the beginning. You didn't like him either."

"Yeah, but we were wrong. He's nice. And if he was around all the time, we wouldn't be so lonesome." He took a big bite of his sandwich.

She wished it was as simple as that. How could she explain things to him without stirring up his grief all over again? She chewed on her lower lip for a moment, then gentled her voice. "Your dad hasn't been gone all that long, Jarrod."

He frowned and stopped chewing. "I know. And I miss him everyday. I'll always miss him. But he's never coming back. I don't think he'd want us to be lonely, do you?"

No, she didn't. Steve had never been selfish. He'd have wanted them both to be happy.

Her son, it appeared, had figured that out a lot faster than she had.

"You're right, honey. Dad wouldn't want us to be lonely. But it takes a long time to get to know someone well enough to marry them."

"How long?"

Not long at all if you were Elijah and Emma. After reading the journals and letters, she'd delved into their backgrounds. They'd married two months after being introduced and gone on to raise three children during their long and happy marriage.

But that kind of rash behavior could also lead to heartache.

"I'm not sure, honey. People just know when the time is right."

"Yeah?" He picked off a piece of crust and popped it in his mouth. "So when do you think you might know?"

Cindy pushed her half-eaten sandwich aside and stood. "I have no idea. Besides, Scott has a say in this, too. He might never like me enough to get married."

"I think he already does."

Her pulse hiccupped. "Why do you think that?"

Wrinkling his nose, Jarrod took another bite. "He looks at you funny. Kind of mushy. Like the people in movies do during the romantic parts, before they kiss each other. Has he ever kissed you?"

Oh, brother.

Cindy grabbed her plate and walked away

from the table. "We're just getting to be friends. It's too soon for kissing."

He inspected her plate as she deposited it on the counter. "Aren't you going to finish your dinner?"

"I'm still full from that pot roast."

The room grew silent. If she was lucky, he'd abandon the topic.

But no. Her son had more to say.

"You know, it's kind of scary to like somebody too much." His voice was quiet. Thoughtful. "'Cause if they go away, it's really hard. But I think it would be worse if you never knew them at all."

She didn't turn. Nor did she answer. She couldn't. Her throat was too tight.

Jarrod, with the infinite wisdom of an eleven-year-old, had homed in on the crux of her issues, giving her plenty to think about.

Like misplaced guilt.

Debilitating fear.

The power of love to linger beyond death.

And he'd also reassured her he was ready to move on, risk or not.

The question was, did she have the same courage?

Chapter Twelve

"Did you drop off Toby this morning?"

"Yes." Scott strolled into Gram's room, circled behind her chair by the window and studied the in-progress seascape. "That's coming along nicely."

"It better be." She cocked her head and gave it a critical scrutiny. "Janice called today to say that young couple bought my painting, and she'd like a few more to display."

Scott grinned and faced her. "Now that's worth celebrating."

She waved off his comment, but excitement had daubed bright spots of color onto her cheeks. "You're in high spirits tonight." She set her brush down and squinted at him.

Yeah, he was. Seeing Cindy this morning, even for a few hurried minutes while he'd handed off Toby, had brightened his whole day.

Not that he was going to tell that to Gram. She needed no encouragement when it came to jumping to conclusions about his love life.

"Things went well at the site. We finished the structural steel."

"Hmph. Never saw you that happy about a bunch of steel before. But different strokes..." She shrugged. "So now you're off to San Francisco."

"First thing in the morning. I'll be in meetings all day, and Mattson wants to have dinner tomorrow night."

"When are you picking up Toby?"

He wandered over to a chair against the wall across from her and sat. "Saturday afternoon."

"I thought Cindy was going to a wedding."

"She'll be home by three."

"Will I see you Saturday night?"

He rubbed his thumb over a spot of dirt on his jeans and switched to evasive mode. "I'll stop in on my way home from the airport instead."

Gram settled back and gave him a smug smile. "You have a date with Cindy, don't you?"

The CIA ought to sign her up for its interrogation team.

He brushed at another speck of dirt on his jeans—this one imaginary. He wasn't ready to share the decision he'd made over the past few days. The one to take his relationship with Cindy to the next level. "Picking up a dog isn't a date."

"Why do I sense there's more to it than that?"

"Wishful thinking?"

Chuckling, she picked up her brush again and twirled it in her fingers. "Don't play coy with me, Scott Walsh. You grew up under my roof. I can read you like a book. But if you don't want to talk about your date with Cindy, fine. I won't pry. I'll just keep praying."

"You've been praying I'd date Cindy?" He frowned at her.

She chuckled again and leaned forward to continue dabbing paint on the canvas. "My prayers are far more ambitious than that. Give me a minute and we can go for a walk. I have a hankering for a few of those Hersey's Kisses. I heard from Devon today, by the way."

He tried to keep up as she hopscotched from one topic to another. "What did she say?"

"Not much, but she sounded upbeat. I thought maybe she'd gotten some part she was after, but she said she hadn't. I couldn't get much out of her. She did ask me to tell you she'd call you soon, though. Did you send her more money?"

"No."

"Odd. She didn't mention needing any this time. When I asked about her finances, she said she had something in the works. I'm not sure what to make of that."

Neither did he. Was it possible she'd taken his advice and sought a job outside of show business?

"There. Enough for today." Gram put her brush in a glass of water and tugged her walker into position. Scott rose to help her up, but she waved him back. "Watch this."

Although it was a struggle, she managed to stand by herself.

Scott gave her a thumbs-up. "I'm impressed."

"So is Brett. He said I'm an excellent student. And I'll let you in on a little secret. I'm planning to ditch this place by Fourth of July."

Scott grinned. "Independence Day. I see Devon isn't the only one in this family with a flair for dramatics. Good for you."

"I still have some things to do in this life." She gripped the handles of the walker and started toward the door. "The good Lord's going to have to wait a while longer to call me home."

As Scott fell in behind her, he sent a silent thank-you heavenward. Not only had his prayers to restore Gram's spirits been answered, but along the way he'd been graced with a second chance at love.

He wasn't going to push Cindy, though. Their situation called for caution and prudence.

But he did plan to move forward—if the lady was willing.

A topic he intended to explore come Saturday night.

"Hey, Mom! I'm going to take Toby out for a walk."

As her son's voice floated up to the second floor, Cindy stepped out of her room and crossed to the railing on the balcony. Jarrod stood in the center of the great room, Toby prancing around at his feet. "Okay, but don't be long. You have to get ready for the wedding in twenty minutes."

"I'm just going to the corner. Then I'll put Toby in the basement." The white ball of fur tugged him toward the door, tongue hanging out in eagerness, and Jarrod took off at a trot behind him.

Cindy smiled. Agreeing to watch the pup had worked out well all around. He'd kept Jarrod entertained Thursday night and all day yesterday while she'd been at work. And starting her morning on Thursday with a quick visit from the pup's owner had been an excellent fringe benefit.

Tonight would be the icing on the cake.

And perhaps the beginning of a whole new chapter in her life.

A shiver of excitement rippled through her as she returned to her room. Scott seemed ready to follow the example of Elijah and Emma—and she wasn't far behind.

She slid the dress she'd selected for the wedding off the hanger. The aqua linen sheath with matching short-sleeved jacket was nice, but she was more focused on her attire for this evening. Scott hadn't said where he was taking them for dinner, but she had a feeling it would be a bit more upscale than the Orchid. Yet she didn't want to overdo it…

Shaking her head, Cindy slipped on the dress. You'd think she was a teenager going out on her first date, with all this dithering over her wardrobe.

She moved into the bathroom to brush her hair, then began applying her makeup. When she finished a few minutes later, she checked her watch. Jarrod was late. No surprise there. Boy plus dog equaled zero notion of time.

Cindy walked over to the window in her bedroom and scanned the street, looking down to the intersection at 101. Jarrod was near the corner—but slowly ambling back. Stretching out his last few minutes alone with Toby.

Just as she started to turn away, a squirrel ran across the open lot at the end of the street. Toby spotted it before Jarrod did, and with an excited bark, he tugged the leash out of her son's hand and took off in hot pursuit.

Toward 101.

And straight toward the car rounding the curve in the highway—visible to Cindy but not to the pup.

If anything happened to Toby...

But her concern about the dog evaporated when Jarrod took off after him.

Because Jarrod couldn't see the car either.

Fear roiling in her stomach, she began banging on the window. Calling out. But he was too far away to hear her.

She had to get the window open.

Hands shaking, she fumbled with the lock, keeping one eye on the running dog, the approaching car and her son.

The sash didn't budge.

She yanked harder.

The car rounded the corner and her pulse skyrocketed.

A moment later, the squirrel ran into its path.

Toby bounded after it.

Even through the glass, she could hear the screech of brakes.

The car began to slide toward the shoulder.

She banged again on the glass, shouting at Jarrod to stay back.

Heard a shattering sound.

Stared in horror as he swerved to avoid the sliding vehicle, then went down when the back of the spinning car clipped him.

Heart hammering, she tore down the stairs and out the front door, the sound of screams following her.

Somewhere in the recesses of her mind, she realized they were her own.

Scott exited the jetway at Arcata/Eureka Airport, resettled his duffel bag on his shoulder and checked his watch. He'd love to call Cindy and chat about their plans for tonight, but the wedding was in progress. Better to ring Gram and alert her he was on his way. The fifteen-mile drive south to Eureka wouldn't take long.

Maneuvering through the throng of exiting passengers, he pulled his phone off his belt, turned it on and saw he had three messages.

Odd.

The construction site was shut down for the weekend, so there shouldn't be any work issues. Gram rarely called, and he'd had a chat yesterday with Devon, who'd been reticent—but upbeat—about her financial situation.

He checked the messages. All three were from Gram, and all had been left during the past hour while his phone had been off during the flight.

If Gram herself was calling, she must be okay.

But something was wrong.

His pulse ratcheted up several notches as he punched in her number.

She answered on the first ring.

"Gram? I just got off the plane. What's…"

"You need to get to the hospital."

He sucked in a breath at her tight, terse tone. "Are you…"

"It's not me. Jarrod's been hit by a car."

Please, God, no!

"Which hospital?" He took off at a fast jog toward the terminal exit.

"St. Joseph's."

"What happened?"

"I don't have any details. Genevieve called me because she didn't have your number." Gram's voice was shaking.

"Okay. We need to stay calm." Like that was going to happen. "Do you have any idea how bad it is?" Scott broke into a sprint toward his car.

"No, but Cindy's there alone. Someone needs to be with her."

"I'm on my way."

"Will you call as soon as you know anything?"

"Yes. Hang in there—and say a few prayers."

"That's all I've been doing since I heard the news."

"I'll join you."

Scott hung up and added his prayers as he sped toward the hospital.

Twenty minutes later, when he charged into the E.R., the nurse behind the intake desk was the same one who'd been on duty the night Gram had been rushed to the hospital. But this time he ran into a glitch. He wasn't family—the key to obtaining information about a patient.

He stumbled when she got to the question about his relationship with Jarrod, then said the first thing that came to mind. "I'm going to marry his mother."

That seemed to satisfy her. She hit the release button for the automatic doors that led back to the treatment area. "Room four."

"Thanks."

Fifteen seconds later, he was on the threshold of the room.

Cindy sat in the single uncomfortable plastic chair, head in hands, shoulders hunched with tension. There were multiple runs in her stockings from the heels up, and her sport shoes definitely didn't go with her classy outfit.

But what freaked him out was the blood. Lots

of it. All over her blue dress. Plus a bulky bandage on her right hand.

No one had told him she'd been injured, too.

Stomach clenching, he approached her. "Cindy." Her name came out in a hoarse whisper.

With a gasp, she jerked and vaulted to her feet, swaying.

Way to go, Walsh. Scare her half out of her mind.

He took her shoulders in his hands to steady her.

"S-Scott? How did you... I thought you were..." Her words trailed off.

She looked liked she was in shock. Her face was white except for the streaks of mascara on her cheeks. Her skin was cold. And she was trembling.

Instead of answering her questions, he pulled her close and folded her into his arms, cradling the back of her head with his hand.

She clung to him, and he heard a sob catch in her throat.

"How is he?" He said the words quietly, against her hair, praying for optimistic news.

"His l-leg is broken. I don't k-know how bad it is. They have him in X-ray now and they're checking him for i-internal injuries."

"What happened? Genevieve called Gram, but she didn't have any details."

"He took T-Toby out for a walk. A squirrel ran by, and Toby got away from him. He took off toward 101. The driver tried to avoid Toby, but the car slid and clipped J-Jarrod."

The dog they were watching for him was the cause of all this.

Scott closed his eyes as a wave of guilt crashed over him, twisting his stomach into a hard knot. "I'm sorry. I should have asked my neighbor to watch Toby."

"No." She backed away slightly and lifted her chin to look at him, her voice stronger. "Jarrod loved having Toby at the house. It was an accident."

That didn't make him feel any better. "What happened to your hand?"

She dismissed the question with an impatient lift of one shoulder. "I was in my bedroom when it happened. I banged on the window to try and warn him, but he didn't hear me. The glass broke. I needed a few stitches. Jarrod's the one who's hurt."

"Walsh?"

At the question from behind him, Scott turned to find Paul Butler once again on duty.

The man did a double take when he recognized Scott. "Are you the fiancé?"

Warmth crept up Scott's neck, and in his peripheral vision he saw Cindy shoot him a startled glance. "A friend. But I needed a ploy to get in."

"Fast thinking." Paul grinned and edged around him to address Cindy. "Let me take another look at that dressing."

"I'm fine."

"A nicked artery is nothing to fool with. You lost a fair amount of blood."

Scott frowned. No wonder Cindy was deathly pale. "How much?"

"Enough." Paul released her hand. "No bleed-through. That's good."

"What about my son?" Once again, panic vibrated through her words.

"He should be okay. No internal injuries. Aside from assorted scrapes and bruises, his primary injury is a broken femur. Otherwise known as the thigh bone. I'll let David Anderson, our resident pediatric orthopedic surgeon, explain the treatment to you." He gestured toward the door as a man with salt-and-pepper hair dressed in surgical scrubs entered. "This is Ms. Peterson, the patient's mother."

Scott moved aside as the man crossed the room, shook her hand and got straight to business.

"He'll need surgery so we can realign the

bone and insert small rods that act as internal splints. He'll be off the leg three to six weeks. We'll remove the rods in about a year. If you agree with that treatment plan, we're ready to go. Any questions?"

Cindy seemed dazed by the rapid-fire briefing. "H-how dangerous is this procedure?"

"There's a possibility of complications with any surgery, but—" the solemn surgeon finally cracked the hint of a smile "—I do dozens of these every year. In my opinion, it's no more dangerous than a tonsillectomy."

Cindy looked at Scott. He reached for her hand but remained silent. He couldn't make the decision for her, but he could let her know he was here to support her, whatever she decided.

"Okay."

The surgeon gave a curt nod. "We'll get started. Someone can direct you to the surgical waiting room. It's more comfortable than this place."

With that, he turned on his heel and exited.

Paul took the man's place. "Not the best bedside manner, but he knows his stuff." He glanced at an unopened container of juice on the tray table beside Cindy's chair, leaned over and picked it up. "Take this along. With her blood loss, she needs to drink fluids." He handed the juice to Scott. Putting him in charge of Cindy's well-being.

And as they followed an aide through a maze of corridors a few minutes later, as he kept Cindy close by his side, he realized he was fine with that assignment. He wanted to be the one she called in times of need, the one she shared her joys and hopes and dreams with.

Bottom line, he wanted her. Period. In his arms—and in his life.

As for any lingering fear holding him back— it had dissipated like an afternoon fog in Starfish Bay as he'd raced to join her at the hospital.

Because this time he knew he'd chosen the right woman.

So once they got past this crisis, he intended to lay his cards on the table.

And pray she'd take a chance on him.

"You need to drink some more."

Cindy lifted her head from her hands in the corner of the surgical waiting room they'd staked out. Scott was holding another carton of orange juice—the second one he'd brought her in the past hour and a half as they'd kept vigil, fingers entwined.

Those were the only two times he'd left her side.

And she'd missed him during both brief absences. Desperately.

Gratitude tightened her throat, and she tried to smile. "I must still look pretty bad the way you keep forcing liquids on me."

"Not bad. Pale." He sat and held out the carton.

He was being kind. During her quick detour to the ladies room on their way here, her reflection in the mirror over the sink had shocked her. Her complexion had been chalky, and the streaks of mascara running down her cheeks had given her a ghoulish appearance. She'd erased those, but there hadn't been a thing she could do about her pallor. And she doubted it had improved much during their vigil in the waiting room.

Her fingers were still quivering, so she grasped the carton with both hands and tipped it against her lips. She hadn't paid much attention to the amount of blood on her dress until they'd arrived here, but after the other occupants had subtly recoiled when she entered, she'd taken inventory—and discovered the reason she'd felt light-headed earlier.

She looked like a victim in a slasher horror movie.

"Thank you. This is helping a lot."

"I wish I could do more." He reached over

and smoothed her hair back from her face, which did nothing to steady the tremble in her fingers. "I called Gram on the way back here. She said to tell you she's praying."

Cindy swallowed. "I appreciate that."

"She asked about Toby, too."

"Oh!" Cindy stared at him. "I'm sorry. I should have mentioned him sooner. He escaped unscathed. Janice is watching him until we can pick him up."

"I'll let Gram know on my next call. Drink some more." He tapped the container in her hands.

She did as he asked.

All the while thanking God for the gift of this man's presence in her moment of crisis— and in her life.

Scott remained silent while she finished off the juice, then tugged the empty container from her fingers, crossed the room and deposited it in a trash bin. When he rejoined her, he gently checked her dressing, as Paul had done earlier.

"I don't see any bleeding. Does it hurt?"

"No. They gave me some shots before they stitched it, and I have pain pills for later if I need them." She looked down at her hand, nestled protectively in his. Feeling more cared for than she had in a long time.

Barbara had told her once, not long after

they met, that she was a capable woman. And she was. But she could get used to having this man, with his quiet strength, in her life. All the time—just as Jarrod had suggested last week, after their tour with Barbara.

Leaning back against the wall, she closed her eyes as her son's other comment from that day replayed in her mind. The one about how it was scary to like somebody too much because if they went away, it would be hard. But as he'd pointed out, it would be worse if you'd never known them at all.

What if the Lord hadn't spared Jarrod today? What if He'd called her son home, as He'd called Chloe home from Elijah and Emma? Would she have preferred never to have had him in her life at all?

No. Of course not. The mother-son experiences they'd shared were memories she would treasure till the end of her days. Despite the pain of loss, she wouldn't have wanted to give up one minute with him.

And she was beginning to feel the same way about the man at her side.

Opening her eyes, she found him watching her, and the warmth, the caring, the tenderness in his expression told her he might have arrived at the same conclusion.

She lifted her uninjured hand to touch his face, to tell him...

"Ms. Peterson?"

At the summons, she snatched her hand back and jumped to her feet. Scott rose, too, and tucked her close against his side.

Dr. Anderson, still in his green surgical scrubs and cap, crossed the room toward them and waved them back into their seats. He dropped into a chair at a right angle to theirs in the corner.

"Everything went fine. As I mentioned earlier, your son will be off his feet for a few weeks, and he'll need some therapy to get his muscles back into condition after that, but he's in excellent shape and I predict he'll bounce back. He's in recovery now, but he'll be waking up shortly. At that point, the nurse will come out to get you so he sees a familiar face as soon as possible. Any questions?"

Cindy sagged against Scott, limp with relief. "Not at the moment."

The doctor rose. "If you do think of some later, don't hesitate to ask one of the nurses or call my office. And don't neglect that hand while you're caring for your son. I heard about your mishap. Keep an eye on those stitches." He included Scott in that instruction.

"We will." Scott spoke for both of them.

Lifting his hand in farewell, the surgeon exited.

With a silent prayer of thanks, Cindy exhaled and stood. "I think I'll freshen up. Not that I can do much about this—" she grimaced as she touched the blood on her dress "—or my stockings. As for the shoes..."

Scott checked out her legs. "I must admit I noticed the shoes."

She grimaced. "I didn't have my shoes on when I saw the accident from the second floor, and I ran out without them. One of the police officers grabbed the first pair he saw, along with my purse, so I could ride along in the ambulance. I'm not exactly making a fashion statement today, am I?"

"I think you look great." He hesitated, as if he wanted to say more, but instead he gestured toward the door. "I wouldn't mind freshening up either, and I want to call Gram and give her an update. Why don't we meet back here in ten minutes?"

"Okay."

They parted in the hallway, but her freshening up amounted to no more than washing her face and hands. A quick check in her purse confirmed that her makeup was still in the bathroom at home. She didn't even have her lipstick.

She was back in the waiting room twice as fast as she'd expected, and five minutes later

Scott appeared with a white sack and two disposable cups in a tray. As he took the chair beside her, the aroma of food wafted toward her—reminding her it was well past lunch time.

"Not as tasty as what you'd have had at the wedding, but it will do in a pinch." He fished out a burger, peeled back the paper and cut it in half with a plastic knife. "That should be manageable. I've had some experience operating with one hand." He flashed her a grin as he settled the burger in her lap.

She felt the pressure of tears behind her eyes. "How can I ever thank you for…" Her voice choked.

"No thanks necessary. Just eat and try to relax until they're ready for us. In the meantime, let me tell you about the great meal I had last night in San Francisco."

Somehow he managed to elicit a soft laugh or two with his humorous, self-deprecating tale about how he'd manhandled his chopsticks in front of Louis Mattson, sending a recalcitrant shrimp flying across the table toward his host's lap. Before she knew it, she'd finished off the burger and downed a sixteen-ounce lemonade.

As he gathered up their trash, a nurse appeared at the door.

"Ms. Peterson?" When Cindy rose, the woman

smiled. "Your son is waking up, and I'm certain he'd much rather see you than me."

She joined the woman at the door and held out her hand to Scott. "Come with me?"

He didn't hesitate. Twining his fingers with hers, he walked by her side as they followed the nurse to the recovery room.

For an instant, Cindy faltered when she caught sight of Jarrod. He looked small and vulnerable and pale against the white sheets, and he was hooked up to far too many monitors. A new wave of fear swept over her.

But then Scott squeezed her fingers, and her strength rebounded.

Together, they approached the side of Jarrod's bed, and she touched his cheek. "Honey? Can you hear me?"

He stirred, then opened his eyes. Blinked. Furrowed his brow, as if trying to focus. "Mom?"

"I'm right here."

"Is Toby okay?"

She smiled. "Yeah. He's fine."

He transferred his gaze to Scott and blinked again. "Is that Mr. Walsh?"

"Yep. I'm here, too, buddy." Scott laid a hand on Jarrod's uninjured leg.

"Did you guys get married?"

A rush of warmth flooded Cindy's cheeks.

"No, honey. We've been waiting here at the hospital while they fixed your leg."

"I guess maybe I dreamed it." He sighed and his eyelids flickered closed. "It was a nice dream. We were at the chapel on The Point. You guys and me and Mr. Walsh's grandma and Nate and Lindsey and the sisters and…well, everyone was there. Even Toby. You had a really pretty dress on, Mom. Pink, I think. And Mr. Walsh had a suit on, with a flower in the buttonhole." He opened his eyes again. "Maybe someday it won't be a dream."

The nurse joined them, checked Jarrod's vitals and smiled. "He's still drifting in and out. Don't be worried if he's not making sense."

Scott put his arm around her shoulders and tugged her close, his breath a warm whisper against her ear. "I think he's making perfect sense. And I also think dreams can come true—if you give them a chance." He urged her around to face him. "What do you think?"

At the tenderness and love shining in his eyes, happiness bubbled up inside her. "I think maybe your grandmother was right all along."

He grinned. "She'll never let us forget it either."

"On the other hand—I'm not suggesting we rush things." Fast might have worked for Elijah and Emma. But she was older. And wiser. And had a lot more baggage—and a son to worry about. "I think we should take it one step at a time."

"I can live with that. So let's take the next step."

He bent toward her, and Cindy met him halfway, melting into the sweetness of a kiss filled with hope and devotion and the promise of a bright tomorrow.

"I know I'm not dreaming now."

At Jarrod's comment, she reluctantly broke contact and turned toward her son, reaching out to take his hand without leaving the protective circle of Scott's arms.

"I don't know, honey." She smiled at Scott. "It feels kind of like a dream to me."

"But it's not." Scott gave her a squeeze. "This is the real deal."

"It sure is." Jarrod beamed at them.

And as Cindy snuggled closer to the man who'd come to Starfish Bay to build an inn but who'd also built a bridge to her heart, she could only agree.

Epilogue

Four Months Later

The black-tie fundraising party for the Humboldt County Historical Society had been a rousing success.

Alone for a rare moment as the event wound down, Cindy smiled as she looked over the dispersing crowd. Based on the numerous compliments she'd received and the comments she'd overheard, guests had been captivated by the life of the late-nineteenth-century sea captain and swept away by his century-old romance—just as she'd hoped they would be.

And judging by the smile on her boss's face as Elaine wove toward her through the thinning horde that had packed the gallery to view "The U.S. Revenue Cutter Service: Patrolling the Coast—and Keeping the Home Fires Burning" exhibit, the director of the historical society was pleased, too.

"I knew when I offered you that promotion you'd excel at the job, but even I never expected anything quite like this for your first effort." Elaine stopped beside her and surveyed the gallery. "I love how you used those blown-up handwritten snippets from the journal, logbook and letters, along with the pictures from Emma's album. They bring the story to life in such a personal way. Not to mention all the wonderful artifacts that were in those trunks."

A flush of pleasure suffused Cindy's cheeks. "It did turn out well. But I had great material to work with."

"I'll say. I especially love the wedding dress." Elaine sighed and studied Emma's gown, displayed in the center of the room on a mannequin in a glass case beside Elijah's jacket and cap. "Such a romantic story. It makes you believe in happy endings, doesn't it?"

At the mention of happy endings, Cindy's gaze swept the room. When she spotted Scott on the far side, looking heart-stoppingly handsome in his tux as he chatted with his grandmother and the sisters from the Orchid, she smiled.

The exhibit wasn't the only thing making her believe in happy endings these days.

"Cindy?"

At Elaine's prompt, she redirected her attention to her boss. "Yes. Theirs was a wonderful love story. And it was inspiring how they stuck together through good times and bad. I'm happy they were blessed with a long, full life and three more children."

"Speaking of children…Anna's about due for a feeding, so she'll be getting cranky. Dave's still nervous about being alone with her, and I promised I wouldn't be gone long. I think he's afraid she'll break if he picks her up." Elaine chuckled and touched Cindy's arm. "Do you mind staying until the end to turn off the lights and lock up? It shouldn't be long. These things wind down fast."

"Not at all. Go feed your daughter."

With a mock salute, her boss headed for the exit.

For the next few minutes, Cindy worked the gallery, thanking departing guests, answering more questions and accepting a few more congratulations. As she finally approached the small group on the other side of the room, the three women beamed at her while Scott gave her a slow, warm smile that kicked her pulse into double time.

"My goodness, Cindy, we had no idea when you told us about this display that it was such a huge undertaking." Lillian glanced around the room. "I can't imagine how you juggled putting this together with all the demands of Jarrod's recovery."

"I had a lot of help from my friends." She encompassed them all with her smile because each of them had pitched in to relieve her of some of her caregiver duties during the past four months. Especially Scott, who had often entertained Jarrod on weekends when she'd come to town to put in extra hours on the exhibit.

"Well, it was worth all the effort," Lillian declared. "I enjoyed every single minute. And what a clever theme."

"I liked the home fires part best." Genevieve smiled, her eyes dreamy. "Talk about a romantic story! I love how Emma always kept a light burning in the window while Elijah was gone. Even though he couldn't see it, he knew it was there. Doesn't that send a shiver down your spine?"

"It certainly does. They were people of such great faith, too. There's a lesson for us all in that, I think," Barbara added.

"Amen to that." Lillian checked her watch. "I do believe we're about to shut down this party, and we have a long drive back to Starfish Bay. I think we'd best be on our way."

"I'll walk out with you ladies and transfer Gram's suitcase from my car to yours." Scott took Barbara's arm.

"You're going back to Starfish Bay with Genevieve and Lillian?" Cindy looked at Scott's grandmother, who'd discarded the walker weeks ago and was about to ditch her cane. It had been hard to keep up with all her activities since she'd moved home on July 3.

"Yes. We're having a slumber party." Barbara nudged Genevieve, and the two of them giggled like teenagers. "Did Scott tell you I'm moving to Starfish Bay?"

Cindy's eyes widened, and she shifted her attention to the tall man who usually kept her up-to-date with all his grandmother's activities. "No."

"That's because I just found out last night." Scott grinned at her. "Since Gram's carrot cake has been such a hit with Orchid customers and her paintings are selling like hotcakes, she's decided to move to Starfish Bay. She's planning to do some baking at the Orchid, paint and help out at the gallery. Janice figures her business is going to increase once the inn opens, and she offered Gram a part-time job there."

"So Genevieve and Lillian and I are going apartment hunting tomorrow." Barbara picked up the story. "I'm going to try it out for a few months, and if I like it, I'll sell my house here and move north."

"You'll love it," Genevieve assured her. She peered over Cindy's shoulder toward the main room. "I think we've overstayed our welcome."

Cindy surveyed the display area. The catering company staff had swooped in the instant the last guest departed, and the servers were stripping and dismantling the cocktail tables and portable serving counters with practiced efficiency.

The three older women hugged Cindy, and Scott took up the rear as they started toward the exit. "I'll be back in a few minutes. Wait for me?"

"No problem. I can't leave until they're done." She gestured to the catering employees.

Truth be told, she wanted a few minutes alone with him. Things had been so hectic from the moment she'd arrived that she'd hardly had a chance to do more than say hello to him. Even when he'd called earlier to wish her luck, she'd been running out the door to drop Jarrod off at Janice's for the evening and they'd exchanged only a few words.

Five minutes later, as the catering crew was packing up the last of the equipment and stowing it in their van, Scott reappeared.

Cindy watched him as he crossed the room

toward her, giving thanks as always for his steady, loving presence in her life. In the past four months, he'd quietly become an integral part of her world—and of Jarrod's. And although she'd entered into this romance with caution, her fears had disappeared. For she had come to believe this was a man she could trust with her life—and her heart.

He stopped in front of her, and his slow, appreciative perusal set her pulses fluttering. "If I haven't already told you, that dress is a knockout."

Smoothing one hand down the fitted black silk skirt that ended at her knees and featured a flirty slit on the side, she touched the pearls at her neck with the other. Despite the dent it had put in her budget, she was glad she'd splurged on the sophisticated dress after she'd spotted it in a boutique window on her drive to work one day a few weeks ago.

If this kept up, however, she was going to become an impulse shopper after all.

"Thank you. You look very nice, too."

He ran a finger under the collar of his starched pleated shirt and gave her a rueful glance. "I appreciate the compliment, but to be honest, I can't wait to get rid of this bow tie. Not to mention the cummerbund. Whoever invented formal clothes was more interested in style than comfort."

"Tell me about it." She lifted one foot and wiggled the skinny high heel on her slingbacks. "Try standing on these for three hours."

"I see your point. But I have to admit I like them." He backed off for a better view of her legs, then gave a soft whistle.

Her cheeks warmed, and she started to turn away. "I need to flip off the lights and lock up."

"Wait." He caught her hand. "Let's take one more look at the centerpiece of your display. It was so crowded in that area, I didn't get a chance to linger over it. And I have some news to share with you, too."

Some subtle nuance in his inflection put her on alert, and she followed in silence as he led her to the glass case containing Emma's wedding dress and Elijah's jacket and cap.

He stopped in front of the display and faced her. "I got a note from Devon today."

That could be good or bad.

"Is she okay?" Last she'd heard, Devon was working full-time as a temp at a theatrical licensing agency in New York while she "explored her options," as she'd put it. But Cindy knew Scott—and Gram—worried about her every day.

"Yes. She's fine. Great, in fact. She just took

a job as manager of a children's theater program with a regional theater company in St. Louis. She'll be teaching kids and directing youth productions, plus acting in some of the main stage productions."

Relief coursed through her, and she squeezed his hand. "That's wonderful! It sounds like a perfect solution. Is she happy about it?"

"I think so. I know it was hard for her to give up her dream of seeing her name in lights on Broadway, but she seems to have made peace with it." He fished in the pocket of his jacket, pulled out a letter and handed it to her. "I got this today."

Cindy released his hand, opened the single sheet of paper and found a check inside. She read the note, which recounted what Scott had already told her…except for the last paragraph.

"I know you've been carrying the burden of Gram's expenses for almost a year, and I'd like to make up for some of that—not to mention my mooching. Please use this to replenish the emergency fund I helped deplete…or for anything Gram needs. There will be more coming down the road. And thanks for all your patience and support. Plus the courage to tell me what I didn't want to hear—that it was time to grow up.

I know that was as hard for you to say as it was for me to hear. I love you, bro. And in case I haven't told you lately, I feel lucky to have you in my life."

A soft smile tugged at Cindy's lips as she re-folded the check into the letter and handed them back. "I agree with that last line."

He returned her smile and tucked the letter into his pocket. "That's encouraging to hear."

With a sigh, she gave the exhibit hall one more scan. "I can't believe the big event is over. At least the display will be up for a few months. Give me a minute to turn off the…"

Once again, he grabbed her hand as she began to walk away.

Looking over her shoulder, she arched an eyebrow in query.

"Actually, I think the real big event is about to begin."

At the sudden huskiness in his tone, her heart stumbled.

He tugged her closer to the glass display case and gestured to the antique wedding gown that had survived for more than one hundred years. "There's something missing from that display, you know."

At his unexpected comment, she frowned and inspected the gown and the grainy, enlarged wedding photo behind it. Emma had worn a wreath of flowers in her hair and carried a bouquet, so of course those were missing. But she'd even found the bride's wedding shoes buried in the depths of the trunk, and they, too, had been restored for the display.

"Okay, I give up. What's missing?"

In silence, Scott reached into his pocket, pulled out his hand and unfolded his fingers to display a Victorian-era engagement ring in pristine condition.

Cindy stared at the round, flat-mounted diamond swimming amid a sea of six violet-blue sapphires that had been cut to form a pointed oval around it. Those stones, in turn, were surrounded by an intricate, filigreed platinum frame featuring additional smaller diamonds. The frame was joined on each side to a gold band to complete the circle.

It was the most stunning and unusual ring she'd ever seen.

And she knew immediately who'd once worn it. She'd noticed it in a few of the photos from Emma's scrapbook.

She looked up at him. "Emma's engagement ring. Where did you get it?"

"Gram inherited it, along with the trunks, but Dad's aunt sent it under separate cover because of its value. Gram's had it in her safe deposit box all these years. She'd totally forgotten about it until you started on this exhibit. She gave it to me a few weeks ago, and I had it cleaned and polished." He paused. Took a deep breath. "Now I'd like to give it to you."

It was a statement, not a question, and he didn't seem to expect her to respond.

Good thing.

She doubted her voice would cooperate.

Without breaking eye contact, he twined his fingers with hers and stroked his thumb over the back of her hand. "I know you want to move slowly. I understand and respect that. You haven't been a widow long, and the last thing you and Jarrod need in your life is more upheaval. I'd planned to take it slow, too, after all the mistakes I made in my last relationship. But I knew from the beginning you were different. And over the past few months, as you've graced my life in more ways than I could have dreamed, I've fallen in love with you."

His voice hoarsened, and one side of his mouth quirked up. "Sorry. I've never proposed before. And in case you have any doubt, that's what I'm doing. I understand if you need more time, but I want you to know I can't imagine my life without you. I want to be like Elijah, confident even when we're apart that you're waiting for me with a light on in your heart, if not in your window. I'm not perfect, as Gram or Devon will be the first to tell you, but I do take my commitments seriously, and I'll work hard to be the best husband and father possible. For always. So if and when you're ready to say yes, I'll be waiting."

As he finished, Cindy felt the pressure of tears behind her eyes and in her throat. "I can't begin to imagine what I've done to deserve the gift of your love." The words came out in a whisper.

The green of his irises deepened to jade, and he lifted his free hand to stroke her cheek. "I'm the lucky one if you love me back."

Once upon a time, Cindy had thought it would take a long time for her to be sure about her feelings for this man.

She'd been wrong.

In the five months she'd known Scott, his kindness and caring and compassion had chased away all her doubts. With his quiet strength, deep faith, absolute integrity and steadfast devotion to those he loved, he'd won her heart. Forever.

She lifted her left hand, touched the ring, then extended the fourth finger. "I'm ready now. And the answer is yes."

Joy filled his eyes—yet he hesitated. "Are you certain? I don't want to rush you."

"I couldn't be any more certain. I love you, too, Scott. So does Jarrod."

In the quiet of the museum—beneath the smiling photograph of Elijah and his bride, surrounded by the mementos of their century-old romance—he cradled her hand in his and slipped the ring over her finger. "How does it fit?"

"Almost as if it was made for me."

"Good. Because it's yours now."

Once more, Cindy looked at the antique wedding gown and the photo of the newlyweds. "I wonder how they'd feel about me wearing this?"

"Gram told me there was a note with it, in Emma's hand. She saved it for you, but she passed on the last line so I could share it when I gave you the ring. It said, 'May some future bride who wears this ring find as much joy and contentment in her marriage as I have known in mine.' So she always intended for it to be passed on. Now—" Scott took her other hand "—given the setting, I think we should seal this engagement in a very traditional, old-fashioned way, don't you?"

Smiling, she stepped into his arms. Where she belonged—for always. "No question about it."

She tipped her head back to welcome his kiss,

and at the tenderness and love in his eyes the rest of the world melted away.

But as he leaned down to claim her lips, she did catch one quick glimpse over his shoulder of that happy couple from long ago.

And as they smiled back at her from the antique wedding portrait, she had a feeling they would approve.

* * * * *

If you enjoyed Irene's book, be sure to check out the other books this month from Love Inspired!

Dear Reader:

Welcome back to Starfish Bay, a charming spot on the Northern California coast that exists only in my imagination—and the pages of my books.

One of the joys of being a writer is creating interesting places and people. Sometimes the place comes first; sometimes the people. With this series, I focused first on place. I wanted a spot that would capture the imagination of readers as much as the setting of my previous series, Lighthouse Lane, did. I've received so many letters from readers who were charmed by that tiny byway on Nantucket Island. I hope all of you who were captivated by Lighthouse Lane—along with many new readers—will fall in love with Starfish Bay, too!

Please watch for the final book in my Starfish Bay series coming next year. In the meantime, I invite you to check my website at www.irenehannon.com for more information about my other books.

Irene Hannon

Questions for Discussion

1. Based purely on the first scene between Cindy and Jarrod, what is your impression of her as a mother? Support your opinion with examples from that scene.

2. By the end of the first chapter, what is your impression of Scott? Did it change over the course of this chapter?

3. Gram says that Scott has an overdeveloped guilt complex. Do you agree? Is guilt a bad thing—or a good thing? Why or why not?

4. Cindy is struggling to juggle the demands of parenting with a full-time job. Do you think she handles this well? What are some of the challenges single parents face?

5. Cindy and Scott get off to a rough start. Why were they able to overcome that and move on? What qualities are helpful in making any relationship smoother?

6. What did you think of Devon? Did your opinion of her change at the end of the book? Why? Have you ever known anyone who refused to take responsibility for his o

her life? What is the best way to deal with a person like that? Did Scott do the right thing when he refused to continue sending her money?

7. What role did faith play in the lives of the main characters in this book? How did it affect their outlook and their choices?

8. Like Scott, Cindy deals with guilt in this book—in her case, for falling in love again so soon after her husband's death. Do you think this guilt was warranted? Why or why not?

9. At the beginning of the book, Gram has given up on life. What happened through the course of the story to lift her spirits? Is there an older person in your life whose spirits need lifting? How might you help raise them?

10. Scott had some fences to rebuild with Jarrod after their antagonistic beginning. What are some of the things he did to win the boy's trust and repair their relationship?

11. Describe the qualities in Cindy and Scott that made them fall in love with each other.

Use examples from the book to illustrate how they demonstrated these qualities.

12. Near the end of the book, Jarrod tells Cindy that it's scary to like somebody too much because it's hard if they go away. But he says it would be worse if you'd never known them at all. Do you agree? What Bible verses might comfort someone who is grieving the loss of a loved one?

13. What is the one thing you will most remember about this book? Why?

LARGER-PRINT BOOKS!

GET 2 FREE
LARGER-PRINT NOVELS
PLUS 2 FREE
MYSTERY GIFTS

Love Inspired®

Larger-print novels are now available...

Love Inspired®
SUSPENSE
RIVETING INSPIRATIONAL ROMANCE

Watch for our series of edge-
of-your-seat suspense novels.
These contemporary tales
of intrigue and romance
feature Christian characters
facing challenges to their faith...
and their lives!

AVAILABLE IN REGULAR
& LARGER-PRINT FORMATS

For exciting stories that reflect traditional values,
visit:
www.ReaderService.com